"ARE YOU POUTING?" ANGIE ASKED TEASINGLY. "Your lower lip is stuck out halfway to Richmond."

"No," Gabe said loftily. "Scientists *never* pout."

She blew a raspberry to show what she thought of that response. "Then you must be pondering over how you came to be stuck with a camera-shy ghost."

"Not funny, Angie," Gabe said, a warning in his voice.

"Yes, it is!"

He grabbed her leg and tickled the sensitive sole of her foot, making her laugh harder as she kicked and squirmed. "Say poltergeist . . . and I'll stop."

"Pol-pol-polter-geist!" she gasped.

Gabe released her foot, only to pull Angie onto his thighs. He pressed a soft, quick kiss to her lips, then moved his mouth a fraction away and whispered, "You're smiling."

"How can you tell?" she whispered back, loving his playful, whimsical side.

"I felt it with my mouth."

"What does my smile feel like?"

"Like you're holding my heart in your hand. . . ."

WHAT ARE *LOVESWEPT* ROMANCES?

They are stories of true romance and touching emotion. We believe those two very important ingredients are constants in our highly sensual and very believable stories in the LOVESWEPT *line. Our goal is to give you, the reader, stories of consistently high quality that may sometimes make you laugh, sometimes make you cry, but are always fresh and creative and contain many delightful surprises within their pages.*

Most romance fans read an enormous number of books. Those they truly love, they keep. Others may be traded with friends and soon forgotten. We hope that each LOVESWEPT *romance will be a treasure—a "keeper." We will always try to publish*

LOVE STORIES YOU'LL NEVER FORGET
BY AUTHORS YOU'LL ALWAYS REMEMBER

The Editors

®644

ANGIE
AND THE
GHOSTBUSTER

THERESA
GLADDEN

BANTAM BOOKS

NEW YORK • TORONTO • LONDON • SYDNEY • AUCKLAND

ANGIE AND THE GHOSTBUSTER
A Bantam Book / October 1993

If you would be interested in receiving protective vinyl
covers for your Loveswept books, please write to this
address for information:

Loveswept
Bantam Books
P.O. Box 985
Hicksville, NY 11802

ISBN 0-553-44343-7

Published simultaneously in the United States and Canada

Bantam Books are published by Bantam Books, a division of Bantam
Doubleday Dell Publishing Group, Inc. Its trademark, consisting of the
words "Bantam Books" and the portrayal of a rooster, is Registered
in U.S. Patent and Trademark Office and in other countries.
Marca Registrada. Bantam Books, 1540 Broadway, New York,
New York 10036

PRINTED IN THE UNITED STATES OF AMERICA

OPM   0 9 8 7 6 5 4 3 2 1

To Rich
with love,
Theresa

PROLOGUE

Ivy Rule woke to the sound of weeping.

She eased up on her elbows, sleepy eyes blinking in adjustment to the lovely silver light of a full August moon spilling into the bedroom through lace curtains. Her gaze searched the room.

On the far side sat the Shadow Lady in a chair that wasn't there. Her hands cupped her cheeks, and she wept copiously. The tears ran down her face and dripped from her dainty little chin. She was very lovely and very young, and she wore an old-fashioned dress made of lace and satin, the kind never seen these days.

Ivy was not frightened of the ghost. She hadn't lived to be sixty without learning that the world was filled with unexplainable things. She was used to sharing her home with this tragic spirit, and Ivy knew the Shadow Lady was not the type of rude ghost that deliberately terrified a soul in the middle of the night.

No, Ivy wasn't frightened, but she was worried. For years, she'd only caught glimpses of the Shadow Lady as she passed through the ornate black-and-gold dining room downstairs, or heard the sound of a piano when there was no piano in the house, or discovered open doors that Ivy had closed only minutes earlier. But of late, the poor lady had taken to waking her up with her mournful weeping, which was so heartbreaking it made Ivy want to cry too.

"Dear lady, you must feel as though your heart is broken beyond mending," Ivy said softly as she sat up. "I wish you could tell me what troubles you."

The Shadow Lady lifted her head. She rose from the chair and drifted toward the bed, hands outstretched as though in desperate supplication.

Ivy slowly lifted her own hands as the apparition came nearer. When their fingers were almost but not quite touching, the ghostly female form began to fade. Ivy could see through her to the door beyond.

"No! Please, wait." Her plea was useless. The Shadow Lady was all gauzy, then gone.

Ivy's mouth was dry from not swallowing. "That poor, dear thing." Her eyes dampened. "No one of flesh or spirit should suffer such misery."

She lay back in bed, listening to the sudden silence reigning over the house and thinking about the man who was coming soon. She prayed he could find some way to help ease the Shadow Lady's eternal heartache.

ONE

Something awaited him inside the old mansion.

Gabriel Richards sensed that the moment the Kingston Inn came into view. A powerful surge of anticipation followed that nebulous notion as he guided his Chevy Caprice into a small lot next to the nineteenth-century mansion that now housed a bed-and-breakfast establishment.

Getting out of the car, he peered at the house through the long shadows cast by the fading September day. It was just as he remembered from his childhood: a magnificent piece of austerity built in an era of gingerbread architecture.

A haunting air of the past still clung to the three-story structure. This house wasn't quaint or inviting like its Victorian neighbors. It was shaped like a massive red-brick box, and the severity of its lines was relieved only by a covered terrace that wrapped around two sides.

His gaze scanned the surrounding grounds and gardens that he'd often roamed as a boy, then returned to the house. He hadn't seen this place since he was twelve, but the passage of sixteen years hadn't changed its aura of deliberate isolation.

The mansion did not sit in plain sight as its neighbors did on the street once known as Millionaires' Row. It sat far back like a lonely orphan, hidden behind a copse of huge magnolia trees, a dense forest of rhododendrons, and a low brick wall that surrounded the three-acre property. Gabriel had always had the impression the house had been built to be a mighty fortress to keep its occupants in and outsiders out.

And it was said to be haunted.

Or so the mansion's current owner claimed. According to Ivy Rule, a female entity that she called the "Shadow Lady" inhabited the Kingston Inn. Mrs. Rule had written Gabriel several months earlier, asking him to investigate the paranormal occurrences going on within her home. He had written back, politely declining for several reasons.

First, he was not a psychic investigator of things that went boo in the night. His work as the assistant director of research at the Institute of Parapsychology didn't include the study of apparitions. Only on rare occasions, when some interesting situation presented itself, did he go ghost-hunting for fun.

Second, at the time Mrs. Rule contacted him, he had been immersed in a fascinating laboratory study. He hadn't wanted to disrupt his work with a gifted young psychic who had an amazing ability to bend metal objects by mental energy.

Third, the site of the alleged haunting was in Danville, Virginia. Gabriel had no reason or desire to return to the quiet town on the bluffs of the Dan River where he had lived the year he was twelve.

A month ago, however, a dream had changed his mind, a busy dream that had been filled with strange glimpses of the past and future.

First he'd seen himself as a boy wandering alone through the overgrown gardens surrounding the Kingston place. The house itself had been abandoned and boarded up, just as it had been when he was a kid. The sun filtered sporadically through the trees, throwing patches of light on the ground near a tumbled-down gazebo at the north edge of the property. Lingering in the air was the scent of flowers, roses in particular. In that place where he used to play, he sensed a terrible sadness. Then he felt himself being engulfed by a shadow. The sound of weeping filled his ears, his mind, his heart. . . .

The scene cleared. In the dream Gabriel saw himself as he was now, a twenty-eight-year-old man, standing beside his car. He was staring at the mansion, feeling that something awaited inside, something good, something he had never experienced before.

Again the scene changed. He was in some kind of hospital room. Two women, sixtyish in age, were there. One of the ladies lay in bed. She smiled and seemed happy to see him. The other shook her head in vigorous disapproval, and the egret feathers on her hat trembled.

Other unfamiliar images crowded into the dream. Through a swirling mist he glimpsed a small boy, a fat tiger-striped cat, and a young woman whose face he couldn't see clearly. Gabriel sensed they were important to him somehow and tried to fight his way through the thick mist to find them. But each time he walked out of the haze, he found himself alone in front of the old mansion.

When he'd awakened from the dream, he hadn't questioned the meaning of it. He had simply accepted that he was being drawn back to that place. The next morning, he had written to Mrs. Rule, accepting her invitation to spend the month of September at the Kingston Inn while he monitored the psychic disturbances.

Gabriel's thoughts were returned to the present by the sound of a car backfiring on Main Street. He felt the afternoon sun branding his back. The smell of freshly cut grass permeated the warm air of late summer.

As he started walking toward the mansion, he again experienced the feeling that something awaited him inside. The feeling grew stronger with each stride. He only hoped that "something" was proof that ghosts did indeed exist.

By the time he reached the steps leading to the front entrance, the air seemed to grow so oppressive, it was difficult for him to breathe. Then he was hit with strong emotional emanations that sped through him in blinding flashes: *Loneliness. Desperation. Despair.*

The psychic impressions lasted no more than a few seconds. He stood motionless for a moment, trying to sort out what he'd felt. The emotional vibrations were old, as old as the mortar holding the mansion's bricks together.

Recovering his equilibrium, Gabriel mounted the steps and halted in the indigo shadows of the covered terrace. He took in the stillness, the coolness. Standing there, he vividly recalled the transient moments of peace he'd found there as a boy when the mansion had been boarded up and vacant.

But according to Mrs. Rule, the peaceful state of her home was now disturbed by a melancholy spirit.

Gabriel turned and rang the doorbell. When no one came after a few minutes, he opened the heavy wooden door. He called out as he stepped inside.

No one answered.

It was cool and semidark in the foyer, which was large enough to be a room in itself. On his left was a black marble-top table and a gilt-framed mirror. White silk fabric was draped across the top of the mirror. On his right was a huge antique desk with a leather-bound guest registry in the center. A couple of chairs and a Victorian settee in wine velvet also graced the area.

He glanced through an arched passage on the left and saw an ornate dining room with a huge crystal chandelier hanging from the ceiling. The room was done in black and gold with touches of white. A white marble fireplace held center stage among two large tables and four smaller ones.

Another arched passage on the right led into a parlor. Large and high-ceilinged, it was brighter than the dining room and decorated with a more feminine touch, with chintz fabrics in shades of soft peach, blues, green, and off-white. Another marble fireplace was the focal point of the room. Sectioned off by oriental carpets were two groupings of comfortable sofas and chairs, as well as various antique pieces and tables.

Gabriel curbed a desire to walk in for a closer look at the Victorian treasures that lent such a romantic ambience to the parlor. There would be plenty of time to explore later.

Going over to the heavy antique desk near the curving staircase, he rang the little silver bell he'd spotted there and waited.

Angie Parker was engaged in a battle of wills with a cat. The cat was winning.

Down on her knees on the kitchen floor, Angie peered behind the refrigerator. Her son's pet had somehow managed to wedge his corpulent body into the tight space between the appliance and the wall.

She was trying to lure the cat out with his favorite brand of tuna, served up just the way he liked it—on one of Aunt Ivy's Wedgwood china plates, with a fresh sprig of parsley on top and a chopped-up dill pickle on the side. But the cat just turned up his nose. Angie couldn't believe he was refusing food. The silly old creature lived to eat.

She sat back on her heels and stared into the cat's strange yellow eyes. "What's gotten into you?"

The cat shook his wedge-shaped head, twitched one large ear, and let out a frightened yowl.

"Don't you dare try to tell me you've seen the Shadow Lady," she scolded. "There's no such thing as a ghost!" She was sick of saying that to her aunt Ivy, to her son Miles, and now to an animal that until recently had shown no neurotic tendencies.

Not that she thought her aunt or her son were neurotic. They were both normal, in their own weird ways. Ivy just had a tremendous imagination, along with a heaping measure of eccentricity. Angie wasn't surprised her aunt thought she could see spirits. Miles's belief in the ghost did surprise her, though. Her little boy had never had much of an imagination. She wasn't sure if she should be pleased or concerned that he'd belatedly developed one at age seven.

Angie sighed. This ghost business had ceased to be harmlessly amusing.

Her patience rapidly eroding, she set the plate on the parquet-tiled floor and stretched one arm toward the cat. Hissing, he went for her wrist with a lightning-fast paw.

She was jerking her injured hand back when a polite masculine voice spoke from behind her. "Excuse me. Could you help me, miss?"

Startled, Angie rocked back on her heels and twisted at the waist to confront the man standing in the doorway between the kitchen and dining room. She wasn't expecting anyone, and she didn't have a clue as to who he might be.

If he had mayhem on his mind, it was hidden beneath a very nice smile. His sharply creased dark trousers, Italian loafers, and crisp white oxford cloth shirt suggested to her that he was an upwardly mobile young businessman trying to look casual but not quite succeeding.

Most likely, he was simply looking for a quiet place to stay the night. Since he was easily the most attractive man to have wandered into Aunt Ivy's bed-and-breakfast during the three weeks Angie had been in charge, it was a real shame she would have to turn him away.

"I'm sorry if I startled you," he said. "I rang the bell out front but no one answered. So I wandered back here." His gaze left her for a moment to travel around the expansive kitchen, with its eclectic blend of stainless-steel appliances and elegant woods.

"I didn't hear the bell." Angie rose to her feet, curiously eyeing the handsome stranger. "Guess I was too busy trying to get Sugar Booger out from behind the refrigerator. If you're looking for accommodations for the night, I'm afraid the inn is closed." The smile that had been edging her lips brightened. "May I direct you to another hotel in town, mister . . . ?"

"No, thank you. The name is Gabriel. Gabriel Richards." He had a wonderful voice. It was several beats quicker than a drawl and marked by a dark velvet tone. "I heard you scream. Are you all right?"

"Sugar Booger just scratched me."

"What is a Sugar Booger?" His gaze didn't waver from her face as he walked toward her.

"My son's cat."

"A cat," he repeated, stopping in front of her. "Is it very fat and tiger-striped?"

"That's Sugar Booger, all right. You must be psychic or something." She laughed.

He stared at her, then a slow grin quirked the corners of his mouth. When the smile reached his silvery gray eyes, Angie immediately felt a tug of attraction. In a world filled with pomposity, humor was a quality she found very compelling.

"Sugar Booger is an unusual name for a cat."

Angie fought an impulse to close the short distance between her and this marvelously virile man. Lowering her gaze from his, she noted the plastic protector of pens and pencils tucked into his left shirt pocket. She wondered if it was still called a "nerd pack."

"He's an unusual animal," she returned lightly, her voice sounding more poised than she felt. "My aunt Clover called my son Sugar Booger when he was a toddler. Miles—that's my little boy—insisted on giving that awful name to the cat."

Gabriel Richards nodded as though that made perfect sense to him. "Why did the cat scratch you?"

"Beats me." She shrugged. "He's not vicious. He's just been acting strange lately. A little while ago, he streaked into the kitchen, yowling as though the hounds of hell had him by the tail. Then he dive-bombed behind the refrigerator. I haven't had any success getting him to come out, and I'm afraid he's going to get stuck."

She wondered at the look of satisfaction that flashed in his eyes. Before she could remark upon it, he said, "Maybe I can get him to come out."

"I doubt it, but you can try." She moved aside.

He hunkered down beside the refrigerator and stretched out a hand. "Come here, boy. It's all right now."

To Angie's surprise, the cat wiggled out and looked up with aloof dignity. He sniffed the hand held out to him, then sauntered over to the dish of tuna and began to eat greedily.

Gabriel rose. As he turned to face the beautiful blonde woman, he tried not to stare, but it was impossible not to. Some women excited men simply by existing. She was one of those women.

He cleared his throat and said, "You say the cat seemed frightened when he ran in here?"

She nodded. "He was so scared, you'd have thought he'd seen a—" She stopped speaking abruptly.

"A ghost?" Gabriel knew that was what she had thought but refused to say out loud. "Animals are said to change behavior in a house that is haunted."

"Don't be silly." She gave him a repressive glance. "There's no such thing as a ghost."

Gabriel rubbed his jaw with one hand, successfully hiding a smile. "You aren't Ivy Rule, are you?"

"I'm her niece. Angie Parker." She held out her hand.

Suspended in another dimension. That was the only way he could describe how he felt the instant his hand closed over hers. Was this the woman whose face he hadn't been able to see clearly in his dream? If she was, he wondered how and why she would become important to him.

He had good hands, Angie observed. Not too big or too small. There was nothing overtly sexual or fawning in the way he held her hand, and she liked that.

"It's nice to meet you, Angie," he said in that dark velvet voice of his. "Do you work for Mrs. Rule?"

"No, I've just been helping her out here at the inn for a few weeks."

Her gaze roved over his face. His features were as appealing as his smile. There was something refreshing about his boy-next-door good looks. Yet quiet power, not innocence, was clearly stamped on his face. His cheekbones were high and wide-set, his jaw firm. His hair was black, clean and shining. Cut to medium length, the inky waves seemed to fall naturally into place.

There was nothing remarkable about his build. He was the wiry kind with good definition and muscle tone. Of medium height, he was no more than a few inches taller than her own five feet six inches. And she liked the way he carried himself, with confidence but without a hint of male arrogance or aggression.

She realized how blatantly she'd been studying him when it occurred to her that he'd mentioned her aunt by name. "If you're here to see my aunt—"

"That scratch needs attention." He raised her hand to examine the angry red welt on her wrist. His expression revealed the same kind of mild concern she felt in response to her son's minor cuts and scrapes.

"It's nothing, Gabe," she told him, feeling rather amused and touched. She tried to pull away, but he held on, his grip firm and determined. "About my aunt—"

"The name's Gabriel." He lifted his head, and for a long moment his fascinating gray eyes gazed into hers. "That scratch definitely needs attention. It's better to take care of it now than to be sorry later."

She shivered when his thumb delicately traveled over her skin just above her knuckles. Half-flustered by her physical reaction to his touch, she didn't protest as he led her over to the sink. She even stood patiently while he turned on the faucets and adjusted the water temperature until it was just right. She could feel his concern in the gentle roughness of his fingertips against her skin as he methodically cleaned the cut.

Angie didn't often find herself feeling shy or at a loss with anyone, especially men, but to her dismay she felt rather awkward with this man. Just for a moment she allowed herself to admit privately that she had been strangely, vitally aware of him from the moment she had looked up to see him standing in the doorway.

"You have a nice sink-side manner, Gabe," she teased. "Are you a doctor?"

"Yes, I am. Not medical, Ph.D." He glanced up to meet her gaze. "But I have to admit, it's kind of fun playing doctor with you."

His warm smile was so beguiling, an edgy excitement began to burn along her nerve endings. She laughed self-consciously, and her free hand came up to push back a long strand of hair that had escaped from her ponytail. As she quickly lowered it, she wondered what it was about him that attracted her so. The humor that gleamed in his unusual eyes? The intense, undeniable intelligence she saw in them too? Or maybe it was the careful and gentle way he was ministering to the scratch on her hand. It was as if he really cared that she was hurt, no matter how slight the injury might be.

"There," he said, patting her hand and wrist dry with a dish towel. "Where do you keep the antiseptic?"

She grimaced. "I hate antiseptic. It stings."

"You'd hate an infection even more."

He was looking at her with an expression she could only describe as puzzled fascination. A blush climbed her fair skin and settled warmly in her cheeks. Good Lord! She couldn't remember the last time a man had actually caused her to blush. Gabriel Richards was certainly having an odd effect on her.

"I'll take my chances."

His long fingers came up to capture her chin. "Anti-septic?" he asked softly.

She held his gaze for a moment while an odd fluttering sensation hit the muscles of her stomach. "Persistent, aren't you?"

He smiled. "Very." He slowly released her chin and dropped his hand back to his side.

She gave a resigned sigh, opened the cabinet nearest her, and took out a small bottle. In short order, he took it from her and liberally sprayed her wrist.

She yelped and pulled her hand away. "Ouch! Darn it. I told you it would sting."

Gabriel leaned against the counter, arms folded, watching as her generous red lips pursed to blow air upon her stinging wrist. "I'll be happy to kiss and make it better."

"I do believe you're a bit of a rascal, Gabe," she scolded, but her eyes laughed into his.

A half-smile lingering on his face, Gabriel studied her. She was beautiful, he thought once again. The delicacy of her features made her look rather ethereal. Her flawless complexion brought to mind pearls and roses. Her face was a perfect oval, her nose a thin straight line. Long Nordic blonde hair was tied loosely at her nape, but several strands had come free to kiss the sides of her face.

Her eyes fascinated him. Arrestingly blue, they were almond-shaped and framed by sooty lashes. A dreamer's eyes.

Somewhere in the back of his mind, he was surprised to feel a synapse click, which meant he recognized her on more than a psychic level. But he couldn't place her. Could she be someone he'd known in the short time he'd gone to high school there? Or maybe someone he'd been introduced to at one of the many boring social affairs given by some patron of the Institute of Parapsychology? No definite answers came to him.

The woman before him was not one he would have easily forgotten, he thought. He'd never encountered a woman who generated the kind of outrageous excitement that Angie Parker did. She was more intriguing and tantalizing than any of the well-bred women he knew.

Certainly none of the academic types he occasionally dated could carry off Angie's flamboyant attire with such warm, feminine grace. Beneath a short black spandex skirt, her long, lithe legs were lovingly outlined by black leggings that ended in lace around the ankles. Ballet slippers showed off her dainty feet. An off-the-shoulder hip-length black tunic was a perfect contrast to her ivory skin and long, slender neck.

He'd heard that psychiatrists said that sex began in the head. One look at this woman and who needed a psychiatrist?

Feeling a bit embarrassed by his carnal reaction, he quickly raised his gaze to hers. Instantly, he was taken aback. Her blue eyes had a coolly amused brightness to them. She looked like she had read every thought that had passed through his head.

She had let him observe her with calm patience, he thought, disconcerted. In fact, he didn't need to be psychic to know she was accustomed to that kind of intense survey. Then she lifted one finely arched brow as though asking if he had finished his appraisal of her physical virtues.

"I apologize for staring so rudely," he said, attempting to redeem himself. "But you look so familiar to me. Have we met somewhere before?"

"I don't think so, Gabe." Her smile widened with warm amusement, and he knew she was thinking he'd just handed her the oldest line in the book.

"Please, call me Gabriel." He was still having a hard time not staring. "I think you're wrong. I'm certain we've met somewhere before."

"Maybe I just have one of those common faces."

"There's nothing common about you."

Her expressive eyes told him he'd just dug himself in a little deeper. "What a sweet thing to say."

"Well, I meant it. Really." He swallowed a sigh. He hadn't felt so socially inept since he was a teenager.

One corner of her beautiful mouth curved upward as she gave him a look of humorous reproach. She leaned closer to run the tip of one beautifully manicured fingernail over his pocket protector.

Gabriel could almost feel the softness of her skin. Her vibrant vitality projected like a launched missile, burning his imagination, flaming desires he hadn't known he could feel so strongly.

"So, Gabe, tell me"—her gaze wandered over his face and throat, then returned to his eyes—"are you in town for business or pleasure?"

The purring quality of her voice rooted around some ticklish zone in his unconscious, making him think of sensual purrs of another kind altogether. He fought a twist of longing as he stared at her, hypnotized by her blue eyes and kissable mouth.

He knew she was flirting with him. Quite deliberately, in fact. In his imagination, he responded in kind, dazzling her with his brilliant wit and winning her undying love.

But that was sheer fantasy. This was real life.

He found it necessary to clear his throat before he spoke. "Unofficially, I'm here on business for Mrs. Rule."

"Oh?" The mouth he wanted to kiss formed a tiny grimace. "She didn't mention anything about it to me."

He answered absently as he traced her lips with his gaze. "I'm staying here at the inn for the month of September. We'll probably be seeing a lot of each other." The last was stated with a tangible note of eagerness that made him wince inwardly.

She stopped fiddling with his pocket protector and dropped her hand back to her side. Not a trace remained of her easygoing, flirtatious manner. Her eyes turned serious. "Gabe, let's straighten things out. You say you're staying *here* for a month?"

"That's right. Mrs. Rule invited me." He suddenly had the feeling that something was off-kilter.

"What is this 'unofficial business' you have with my aunt?"

"I'm investigating the paranormal occurrences Mrs. Rule claims she has experienced. I assume she's told you about the ghost she calls the Shadow Lady?"

"Oh, my Lord," Angie breathed.

Gabriel watched a stunned look spread across her lovely face. He could feel her emotions slowly shifting and changing toward him.

Her stunned expression faded, leaving her gaping at him as though he were a two-headed freak in a side-show. And he knew her previous interest in him had just dropped to zero.

He sighed inwardly. Sometimes it wasn't much fun being psychic.

TWO

Angie quickly recovered and closed her gaping mouth. "Okay. This is a joke. Right?" She managed a sporting grin. "Who put you up to it? I bet it was Jake. Of course. He's getting back at me for telling him the doctor said Nila was going to have triplets. Oh, you should have seen his face. It was the personification of mortal fear!"

"I'm not playing some kind of prank."

"Jake didn't send you?"

He crossed his arms and returned her steady gaze. "I'm not acquainted with anyone named Jake."

"You really are a . . . a ghostbuster?"

"I'm a parapsychologist."

"It's the same thing, isn't it?" she asked, unconsciously taking a step back.

"No. It isn't." He shoved his hands into his pockets and leaned against the cabinet behind him. "Since the movie *Ghostbusters* came out, many people have formed the mistaken impression that *all* parapsychologists do is hunt specters. Actually, very few of us do that sort of thing these days."

"But you do."

"Occasionally. I spend most of my time in a laboratory studying other types of psychic phenomena."

Angie eyed him warily. He looked so nice, so normal, so . . . darn appealing. But he was obviously nuttier than Aunt Clover's Thanksgiving pecan pie.

An article she'd read recently suddenly came to mind. With growing alarm, she wondered if he could be one of those phony psychic investigators who capitalized on the gullibility of wealthy old ladies to gain access to homes filled with valuable paintings and antiques. They were con men who robbed their victims of anything and everything valuable.

She couldn't stop herself from blurting out, "If you've come here thinking you're going to get a penny out of my aunt, think again!"

Gabriel was too startled to reply for a moment. This blonde, blue-eyed honey of a woman thought he was a crook! No wonder he'd sensed a rapid rise in her emotional temperature. He supposed he ought to be offended, but he wasn't.

"I think you've jumped to the wrong conclusion," he said evenly. "That's understandable. Suspicion and skepticism are attitudes I often encounter in my profession. I don't like it, but it comes with the territory."

She didn't look convinced. "So you say. My aunt

isn't a wealthy woman. One charming con man already swindled her out of her life's savings."

"I'm sorry. It's unfortunate that your aunt was victimized by an unscrupulous person. I can assure you I have no designs on her money or possessions." He paused, studying her expression. "You don't believe that, do you?"

"I don't know what to believe right now."

He crossed his arms over his chest and offered up the best smile he could find. "The crooks and crazies have made it difficult for sincere scientists like me. I'm not out to defraud your aunt. Honest."

"Oh, sure. Like you'd really admit it if you were."

"Now, how do I argue with that?"

"You don't." Angie was dismayed to feel a flood of warmth at the glint of humor in his eyes. Wasn't it just her luck that the first truly interesting-looking man she'd met in ages was a nut or a crook . . . or possibly both.

"It would be best for all concerned if you left now." Frustration tightened her voice. "Go home, Gabe. Forget about investigating anything around here."

He shook his head, still smiling. "I made a commitment to Mrs. Rule. And I never turn my back on a commitment."

"You're really serious about this, aren't you?"

"Very." His nice smile stayed firmly in place.

She closed her eyes in exasperation for a second. "How does one *scientifically* hunt ghosts?" she asked, reluctantly giving in to curiosity.

"Research methods used in parapsychology are the same as those employed in the social sciences," he answered patiently. "We also apply high-technology methods. I use the high-tech tools of the physical sciences to study evidence that proves or negates the existence of apparitions."

Slick answer, Angie thought. Very intelligent and articulate. It even made sense to her. But she wasn't willing to trust him simply because he had an innocent face, a great smile, a whole lot of brains, and more than his share of sex appeal.

" 'Tools of science'?" she said, deciding out of desperation to go on the offensive. "Is that what they're calling tarot cards and crystals these days? What's your gimmick, Gabe? Seances? Ghost exorcisms? Hocus-pocus?"

She couldn't help feeling a little ashamed of herself as she met his blank stare. It wasn't like her to be so insulting, but she didn't know what else to do. Someone had to be responsible for protecting Aunt Ivy from foolishly involving herself with a ghostbuster.

"Are you rude to everybody?" he asked. "Or just to me?"

Surprise widened her eyes for a second, then she smiled. The smile grew into an appreciative laugh. She hadn't expected him to challenge her, but she admired him for it.

"Just to you. Normally, I'm very sweet-natured."

She laughed again, but as he smiled back, her merriment faded. She wanted to kick herself. She couldn't believe she had just stood there laughing and trading goofy smiles with a man she wanted to get rid of.

Outright insulting him obviously wasn't accomplishing that goal, she thought, sighing. It was only making her feel petty.

Wondering what her next move should be, she walked over to the Shaker-style table and sat down. She fished around in her purse for a gold cigarette case and lighter. She'd been trying to quit completely for almost a year, but she still picked up a cigarette whenever she was bored or nervous. Ivy's latest folly was making her very nervous indeed.

"Those things are bad for you," he chided from across the room.

She gave him a mind-your-own-beeswax look as she took her first puff.

Potential trouble in the form of Gabriel Richards came walking toward her. She frowned, noticing how the cat lazily followed him. The indolent creature rarely exerted himself for anyone but Miles. It was puzzling that the animal had taken such a liking to a stranger.

Gabriel sat down across from her. The cat slipped under the table and curled up at his feet.

Angie clamped her lips together to hold back the automatic social grace of offering him a beverage. Southern hospitality was inbred to the bone, and it died hard.

"Mr. Richards—"

"It's doctor, actually. Ph.D. as I mentioned. But please, call me Gabriel."

"Whatever. Look, the bottom line is that my aunt does not own the Kingston Inn. I do." Angie's name was on the mortgage, but she didn't really consider the house hers. He didn't need to know that, though.

"Really?"

"Ivy had dreamed of owning a bed-and-breakfast inn for years. After Billy Ray Johnson skipped town with practically every cent she had, Ivy couldn't afford to finance the business on her own."

"So you made her dream come true. You love your aunt very much."

"Yes, I do." She was momentarily disconcerted by the way he was smiling at her. Lord! Why did he have to have such a great smile? "As I was saying, Ivy wouldn't let me just give the house to her. She insisted that I become her business partner."

"You've preferred to be a silent partner," he said, regarding her thoughtfully. "Until now. You feel this situation leaves you no choice but to pull rank, so to speak."

"That about sums it up."

He propped one elbow on the table and rested his chin in the palm of his hand. As he stared intently at her, Angie had the uncomfortable notion he was analyzing and cataloging the inner workings of her mind.

"The inn's profit doesn't concern you, does it?"

She angled her head, looking at him in surprise. "It isn't my top priority."

"Your only interest is that your aunt enjoys running it, that it makes her happy."

Startled by his accurate assessment, she answered only with a nod. How did he know that? Lucky guess?

"Has Mrs. Rule discussed with you the odd occurrences she's experienced?"

"She has."

"How reliable is she?"

Angie frowned. "If you're tactfully asking whether she's snapped her garters, she hasn't. Ivy isn't crazy or senile. She's just . . . imaginative."

"If you think your aunt has simply imagined this Shadow Lady, then why not allow me to prove that it's only her imagination at work?"

"Because for all I know you could be a—" She stopped abruptly.

"A con man?" he finished for her.

She didn't respond. It was becoming difficult for her to picture him as one of those crooked psychic investigators she'd read about. He had that Boy Scout look about him: sincere, honest, trustworthy. Of course, she supposed a con man who couldn't successfully mimic those qualities ended up becoming closely acquainted with big, hairy jail cell mates named Bubba, but the nagging doubt that he wasn't a swindler persisted.

"Okay, maybe you really are harmless," she said in an irritated tone.

"No man likes to be described as harmless."

His eyes took on a heated, sensual look as his gaze

held hers, and she felt her body reacting to that look. There was a tingling sensation in her breasts and in the muscles deep within her feminine core. Fool! she called herself as she fought a warm billowing of desire.

"You're a ghostbuster," she said, more as a reminder to herself. "I don't trust anyone who dabbles in paranormal stuff. It's too ridiculous for a rational person to take seriously."

He grinned, seeming undaunted. "You like for things to make sense, don't you?"

"Well, of course."

"I'll bet you're a type-A personality too. Smoking is a nervous habit, you know."

"My habits are none of your concern."

"Don't you want someone to be concerned about you?" The tone of his voice was so gentle, it took her aback.

"I'm perfectly capable of taking care of myself."

"I wasn't suggesting you weren't. Only that . . ." His voice trailed off as though he'd thought better of what he'd been about to say.

He stretched his hand across the table and ran his index finger over the initials APS worked into the top of the elegant gold cigarette case. Angie averted her gaze from the slow, sensual way his finger traveled over the last curved letter.

"What does the *S* stand for?" He stared at her as though the fate of the free world rested upon her answer.

Intrigued by such intensity, she wondered what it

would be like channeled into passion. That thought sent an involuntary shiver traveling up her spine.

"Superwoman." She hadn't meant to say that in a sweet and teasing voice, but she had. Rats! Why couldn't she maintain a cold and aloof manner toward him?

"I believe it." He smiled and she couldn't help noticing that smile was as slow and sensual as the movement of his finger upon the gold case. "You intrigue me," he added so softly, she wasn't certain she'd heard him correctly.

"Do I?" Her hand trembled slightly as she flicked ashes from the glowing end of the cigarette. His gaze tracked the movement.

"Am I making you nervous? Or is it my profession that you find unnerving?" He smiled beguilingly. "There's no need for you to be wary of me."

"I'm not," she said, shuttering her eyes to hide the lie. She *was* wary of his profession, but it was the man himself who disturbed her in ways she didn't want to examine too closely.

She looked up to meet his gaze. "What is it going to take to get you out of our lives?"

"I beg your pardon?" He was clearly startled.

"Whatever my aunt is paying you to investigate this ghost nonsense, I'll double it. All you have to do is get back in your car—"

"And get the heck out of Danville?"

"That's right."

"I liked you better when you were flirting with me."

Angie felt her cheeks grow warm. She hadn't blushed so much since her adolescence. "It was nothing personal," she responded as casually as she could manage. "I flirt with everyone."

"How demoralizing," he said softly, his eyes making contact with hers in a way that defied her to look away. "For a while there, I thought we were hitting it off."

"We're not hitting it off at all." She shook her head as she extinguished the cigarette.

He was silent, then said, "I'm afraid you're right." She heard a note of disappointment in his voice, and privately admitted to feeling the same way.

If only . . . Forget it, she told herself. She couldn't afford to become sidetracked by hormones.

"You haven't answered my question," she said. "How much?"

"You're seriously offering me money to walk away from the commitment I made to Mrs. Rule?"

"Yes. Name your price."

Life had taught Gabriel to expect the unexpected. Angie Parker's offer of cold cash was as unexpected as his intense attraction to her. He felt himself losing his grip on his temper and made an effort to control it. Only a slight stiffening of his shoulders betrayed his inner tension. "I have no financial arrangement with your aunt. Other than room and board while I investigate the baffling phenomenon Mrs. Rule has experienced, I do not expect monetary compensation for my time and expertise."

"Oh, bull dooty. Do you really expect me to believe that you're offering your services out of the goodness of your heart?"

"No. I hope to be rewarded—by finding evidence that ghosts exist."

She slammed her fist down on the table. "I am sick to death of this ghost business! They exist only within the vivid imaginations of those who *want* to believe they have seen them. The Shadow Lady exists only in my aunt's *imagination*."

He shrugged. "You're entitled to your opinion. But you know something, Angie? A little skepticism is healthy; too much is corrosive."

"You don't understand. My aunt doesn't have anyone but me to look out for her."

"Angie, if it will relieve your mind, call my superior at the Institute of Parapsychology in Durham, North Carolina. He'll vouch for my character. I don't swindle gullible widows. I'm a *researcher*, and I specialize in the fields of extrasensory perception and psychokinesis."

She arched a brow. "What is that psycho thing?"

"Psychokinesis. The movement of objects by mental energy, or the power of mind over matter."

"Ooo-kay, if you say so." She frowned and folded her arms beneath her breasts. "And I suppose you think you have ESP or that psycho whatever."

"I do possess some clairvoyant ability," Gabriel admitted. He doubted she would believe him, but he refused to deny what and who he really was.

Her mouth turned up in a smile that was a shade too smug to suit him. "I knew you were going to say that. Does that make me clairvoyant too?"

"No. What it makes you, in my opinion, is a pain in the butt!" The words seemed to burst from him, and he felt his eyes go wide with astonishment. An apology died on his lips when she started laughing. He found himself joining in.

"You shocked yourself with that zinger, didn't you, Gabe?"

"Sorry about that."

"I fired the first insulting shot. I don't mind you shooting back."

"I like you, Angie Parker." Again he was astonished. He hadn't meant to say that either.

He watched all traces of amusement fade from her dreamy eyes. She stared at him. He stared back. They were like two jaguars, he thought, suddenly coming across each other in the jungle. Jittery. Wary. Circling each other, trying to decide whether to attack or retreat without losing dignity.

Adrenaline raced through him. He could feel it in her too. Tension, primal and sexual, crackled between them as if it were a living thing.

What was happening to him? Instead of lusting after this erotically sexy beauty with a bad attitude, he ought to be saying to hell with her. It ought not to matter to him that she thought he was up to no good.

He broke the silence first. "Mrs. Rule is expecting

me," he said firmly. "Before you overrule her decision in having me here, perhaps you should direct me to her."

"She isn't here."

"I'll wait for her to return."

Conflicting emotions crossed her face. "Ivy tripped and fell down the stairs three weeks ago. She's in a nursing facility, recovering from surgery on her broken hip. She was chasing that damned imaginary ghost when she fell."

"The woman in the hospital bed," he murmured, lowering his gaze. One by one the fragmented pieces of his dream were coming together and becoming a reality.

"What did you say?"

"Nothing. Our arrangement was made over a month ago. I wasn't informed of her accident. I'm sorry. How is she doing?"

He glanced up at Angie as he spoke. She looked upset and in need of comfort, and he was hit with an unexpected urge to hold her hand in an effort to provide that comfort. Before he acted on that impulse, he reminded himself that she was still suspicious of his motives. He clasped his hands together on the table surface.

Angie felt oddly soothed by the compassion she saw in his eyes. "Thank you. Her doctor feels very positive about her recovery. She is in excellent health for a woman her age." She managed a tiny smile. "Aunt Ivy normally has more energy and bounce than a cheerleader having a good hair day. Nothing keeps her down for long."

"I look forward to meeting her. Have you managed the inn since her accident?"

"Yes. Guests were staying here at the time, and several more were expected in the following weeks. So my son and I temporarily moved into the house. Fortunately, the last guest left this morning. I've canceled reservations through the first of the year and, as of today, the inn is officially closed."

"You sound happy about it."

"I'm thrilled. Innkeeping isn't my thing. I'm looking forward to the privacy of my own home and to getting back to my job."

Angie went silent, realizing she was talking too much, telling him things she hadn't intended to. Maybe it was just too hard to repress her natural tendency to be chatty and friendly. Or was it because he seemed so interested in whatever she had to say?

He smiled encouragingly. "What do you do when you're not being a reluctant innkeeper?"

"I work part-time in a combination book, gift, and gourmet food store that my friend Nila Madison owns. I started working there just to help out, when Nila first opened the store. She needed me because she was operating on a shoestring. The store has become very successful, so I'm more or less her assistant manager now."

Again, she fell silent. What was wrong with her? She should be concentrating her efforts on getting rid of this charming but nutty ghostbuster, not palavering with him as though he were a new friend.

Apparently he'd decided she'd told him enough about herself, too, for he brought the conversation back to the problem at hand.

"Don't you think it's odd that Mrs. Rule didn't let me know about her accident? That she didn't cancel our arrangement?" he asked.

"Not at all. Ivy's the sweetest person on earth. But she can be real stubborn when she gets hold of an idea."

"Then why didn't she tell you to expect me today?"

"Probably for the same reason she didn't tell me about you at all."

"She knows you don't approve."

"Exactly."

"She didn't want you to talk her out of the investigation."

"Right." Angie sat back, crossing her legs with an aloof nonchalance she was far from feeling. It was becoming more difficult by the moment to keep her defenses solidly in place. She was too aware of him, in every way a woman could be aware of a man.

He really did make her extremely nervous, which was a new experience for Angie. From the cradle, she'd had a knack for dealing with the male of the species. She couldn't remember a time when she couldn't bring a man around to her way of thinking with a smile, or turn one into a willing slave with the merest flirtation.

Gabriel Richards was different, though. She couldn't get a handle on how to deal with him. That alone sent up red flags telling her to be on guard.

"We've reached a stalemate, haven't we?" he said.

She nodded. "I'm afraid so."

"Phone Mrs. Rule," he suggested. "Talk to her. If she agrees with your decision to terminate our arrangement, I'll apologize for bothering you and be on my way."

"Fair enough." Angie got up and walked to the telephone.

A short conversation confirmed everything Gabriel had told her. Ivy sounded so thrilled—so much more like her perky, cheerleader self than she had in months—that Angie didn't have the heart to scold her for committing such an excessive folly in contacting a ghostbuster and keeping it secret from her. Nor did she have the heart to refuse Ivy's request to see Gabriel.

"Ivy wants to see you," she told him grudgingly as she returned to the table.

"When?"

"Tomorrow morning." She fell into a chair and threw her hands up in the air. "Weird. This whole thing is just plain weird."

"Weird is relative," Gabriel remarked mildly.

"You're telling me. *All* my relatives are weird." She sank her brow into her palm. "Aunt Ivy sees ghosts and believes that plants have feelings. My Aunt Clover hates men, wears her dead sister's hats, and buys her clothes from thrift shops, even though she has more money than the Queen of England. My beautiful, elegant mother and financial-wizard father are tooling around Russia on a Harley-Davidson to observe the effects of the decline of communism." She couldn't help smiling as she looked up at Gabriel. "The last time I heard from them, they were sipping vodka and eating black-market caviar with an ex-CIA agent and his wife, and being entertained by the ex-agent's tales about the 'good old days.' And then there's . . ." Her voice slowly trailed off.

Gabriel watched her eyes cloud. He sensed that some member of her unusual family caused her more distress than she wanted to talk about.

She seemed to shake off whatever was troubling her. Her chin went up and she spoke firmly. "I dearly love each and every one of those wonderful, eccentric people. And I would do anything within my power to protect them. So just because I've agreed to take you to see Ivy, don't get the wrong idea. I still intend to talk her out of this ghost nonsense."

"I understand."

"Whatever happens, I don't want you encouraging Ivy to believe this thing is real. It isn't real. It *isn't* real."

He regarded her solemnly. "It isn't my intention to foster anyone's belief in ghosts. My job is to be objective. All I want to do is gather evidence that will either prove or negate the existence of something paranormal going on in this particular place."

He reached out and covered her hand with his, and felt a shock of awareness charging through his body. "I understand your need to protect your aunt," he said in a gentle voice. "If the situation were reversed, I would probably feel the same way. All I'm asking is that you reserve judgment. Give me a chance to prove that I'm not a threat to you or your family."

"Don't." She pulled her hand away.

Sensing that wariness in her again, he resisted the urge to recapture her hand. "What if you're wrong? What if there is something unexplainable going on here?"

She shook her head. "I don't want to discuss it anymore. In fact, I think it would be best if you left now." She pushed her chair back and stood up. "There are several nice hotels in town. I'm sure you'll be able to find suitable accommodations for the night in one of them."

He sat looking at her for a moment, then reluctantly got up. "Where and what time do we meet tomorrow?"

"Here. Ten o'clock."

He nodded and started out of the room, not paying any attention to the cat trailing after him. He was almost through the doorway when he stopped in his tracks.

The eerie sense of familiarity returned to him.

Why did Angie seem so familiar to him?

He slowly turned. She was watching him, her stance bold, one small fist tucked into the curve of her hip, her face a mask of distant politeness.

He knew her.

The feeling was as persistent as the tension swirling the air around him.

"I know I sound like a broken record, but I swear we have met before."

"Honestly, Gabe." She laughed, the sound forced and hollow. "I'm certain we've never met. Now, do be a good little boy and run along."

Her last words caused echoes of his past to come tumbling back to him: Danville High School; laughter skipping through halls that smelled of some cheap industrial disinfection mixed with the sweat of damp gym clothes stuffed in gunmetal-gray lockers; Mrs. Adams's geometry class; his first crush on a blue-eyed beauty with a smile that could take him to the clouds and whose rejection could cut like broken glass. For a moment he was incapable of movement, of speech. . . .

Gabriel roused himself from the place where thoughts, memories, and fantasies dwelled. "Angie Sinclair," he said, unable to keep a painful note of awe out of his voice.

She looked startled. "How did you know my maiden name?"

"You probably don't remember me. Our paths crossed briefly in high school." He drew in a deep breath, hesitating. Was it best to let sleeping memories lie? He saw curiosity replace the suspicion in her eyes, and he knew it was too late to stop this thing he'd started.

"I don't remember you." She tipped her head to one side, looking at him consideringly. "You really lived here in Danville? We went to school together?"

He nodded. Suddenly not knowing what to do with his hands, he stuck them into his pockets. "I was only here for a year. We moved frequently, because my parents were consulting engineers. We came here so they could work the kinks out some new machinery at the textile mills."

She searched his face as though looking for some sign of recognition. Obviously, none came. "I still can't place you. I'm sorry."

"I'm not surprised," he said. "I was very small for my age. Skinny to the point of being all arms and legs and eyes."

"What class were you?"

"I was a freshman like you." He smiled. "I remember you were the prettiest and most popular ninth-grade girl at Danville High. I sat behind you in Mrs. Adams's geometry class."

"No, you're wrong." Angie laughed and rolled her eyes. "The kid who sat behind me was this brainy little nerd who worshiped his slide rule, always had a pocket protector full of mechanical pencils, and never failed to ruin the class grading curve for everyone else. We used to call him . . ." Her voice trailed off as realization hit her.

THREE

"The Geek," Gabriel finished for her.

Angie cringed in embarrassment for not recognizing him in time to stop the words she'd spoken, for inadvertently reminding him of youthful cruelties.

Her mind flashed back to the unusual boy she'd known so briefly. Too little, too smart, too serious, Gabriel Richards hadn't fit into any of the high school subcultures. He had been two to three years younger than his fourteen- and fifteen-year-old classmates. The difference in age, inconsequential in adulthood but monumental in youth, had set him apart. The popular crowd had treated him as a joke. Even the "brains" had considered him an oddball misfit because of his spooky intensity. In the unwritten rules of teenage social behavior, to openly accept him as friend would have been instant social suicide.

Angie forced herself to stop staring and speak. "I do remember you now. I'm sorry for what I said."

"Water under the bridge." He responded so graciously that she felt embarrassed again. "We were study partners in geometry class."

"That's right."

The years had been more than kind to him, she thought. His face and his body had filled out, and thick-lensed glasses no longer hid his arrestingly attractive eyes. He wore contacts now, she supposed.

"Mrs. Adams stuck you with me when she divided the class into pairs," he reminded her. "Everybody thought that was hilarious." He held her gaze, his look evaluating and introspective. " 'Beauty and the Geek.' Isn't that what they used to call us?"

Angie tried not to wince, but wasn't successful. "You—" She shook her finger at him. "*You* were the one who was stuck with *me*, the math dummy."

He smiled at that. "Don't get polite on me now, Angie. We both know you weren't dumb. I never could understand why you didn't want anyone else to know you had a brain."

"I learned at an early age that nobody expected me to be smart." A self-conscious laugh escaped from her throat. "Dumb blonde, that's how people saw me. They still do, as a matter of fact."

"Strange, isn't it, how we tend to put labels on each other?"

"Yes. It's so unfair," she said softly.

He responded with a smile. "You are one of the few people I remember from that year. I think it's because

I hadn't paid much attention to the differences between boys and girls until Mrs. Adams made us study together." His smile became wry. "I had a wicked crush on you. I used to make up excuses to talk to you every day after the last class period." And he remembered one time with crystal clarity.

It was the last time he'd cornered her at her locker after school. All week long, he'd worked up his courage to ask her to go to the freshman spring dance with him. The speech he had painstakingly prepared had gone right out of his head the moment he was alone with her. He had stammered and blushed four shades of red without getting to the point. To make matters worse, he'd tried to be a gentleman by helping her with her books, but had only succeeded in dropping one on her foot and slamming his finger in her locker. She had called him a "poor little boy" and had suggested he stop by the nurse's office to make sure his finger wasn't broken. He'd known then that Angie would never look upon him as a potential date, or even as an equal. He had walked away without ever asking her to the dance.

Gabriel watched her lift a hand and begin rubbing her arm at the elbow in an almost unconscious gesture of nervousness. Glancing at him, she gave a small, humorless laugh. "I wish I had been nicer to you then." Her voice was soft, almost as though she were talking to herself, and her eyes stared blankly at something only she could see.

Her simple but poignant statement caught him off

guard. Some people might have said, "Gee, Gabriel, you sure have changed." Others might have laughed and launched into stories about "the good old days." For some reason, he felt obligated—no, he *needed* to reassure her that he did not harbor any leftover resentment or ill will. "Hey, don't worry about it. Ninth grade was a million years ago. Kids can be—"

"*Unmerciful.*" She spoke the word with a bitter edge. "The world is pitilessly intolerant of anything or anyone different."

He stared at her for a full ten seconds, realizing she had retreated somewhere inside herself. His first inclination to soothe and comfort faltered, because he was puzzled. What did the confident, poised beauty he remembered know of the pitilessly intolerant attitude some people had toward anyone different?

He rocked back on his heels and his gaze lowered as he wondered what, if anything, there was left for them to say to each other. Then it occurred to him that he was experiencing self-consciousness for the first time in years.

Psychic awareness combined with a high IQ had made relationships difficult for him as a child. Never staying in one place long enough to grow roots hadn't helped either. His early years had been lonely, often painful and frustrating, and sometimes very frightening. It wasn't until his parents had finally allowed him at age thirteen to attend a school for gifted children that his life had begun to change for the better.

Since then, he had worked through the problems of being different. He had acquired a social polish that allowed him to be comfortable interacting on a surface level with people. That, he decided, was the key word: "surface." Ninety-nine percent of his relationships were easygoing, friendly "surface" relationships.

"So, Angie Sinclair Parker," he said, when the silence had grown uncomfortably awkward. "You grew up beautifully."

"Thank you." She seemed to come back from the journey inside herself, and a smile touched her lips. "You grew up rather nice yourself."

He returned her smile. "You've obviously married."

"I'm a widow. I have a seven-year-old son named Miles." She hesitated as the shadow of some emotion passed over her face. "What about you? Do you have a wife? A family?"

"No wife. No family. Except for my parents, that is."

For a moment neither of them spoke, then Gabriel raised one hand in a farewell salute. "May the Force be with you," he said, trying to infuse a little lightness as he departed.

She lifted a delicately arched brow. "*Star Wars*?"

"Maybe." He grinned, then his expression grew solemn. "I'll be seeing you, Angie Sinclair Parker."

He strode off through the dining room.

Angie hugged her arms to herself, watching him until he was out of sight. In her mind's eye, she kept seeing the boy Gabriel. A friendly smile and a few kind words would have meant so much to that young boy. She had never been deliberately mean to him, as others had; she had simply treated him as a mild annoyance, ignoring him whenever possible. She wondered sadly now if that hadn't been worse than outright meanness. Regret filled her for withholding a friendship she could have offered so easily. Along with this belated sense of compassion came a deep feeling of shame.

What goes around comes around, she thought with grievous irony. Her own child was now suffering a similar unkind fate at the hands of his callous peers.

The past was something she could not change. But the present . . . she could do something about that.

She took a deep breath, drew on her reserve of courage, and went after Gabriel.

The front door wouldn't open.

Gabriel was vaguely aware that the cat stood beside him, swatting at the hem of one pant leg. All that really registered, however, was that the damn door wouldn't open. His heart striking a faster rhythm, he gripped the doorknob with both hands and poured all his strength into turning it clockwise.

Nothing happened.

Then a feeling jolted him, a feeling that almost staggered him to his knees.

He held on to the brass doorknob and leaned against the door for support. His feet itched to move, but he was rooted to the spot. As though struck by lightning, he then went blind for a flash.

There was someone in the foyer with him.

He felt the presence as surely as he felt the hammering of his heartbeat and the beads of sweat across his brow. It wasn't the cat whose presence he sensed, though some part of his mind registered the steady drone of the animal's plaintive yowl and the frantic clawing at his pant leg.

The presence grew stronger, seeming to invade his every pore. All sound receded until there was only a buzzing in his ears. For a moment his raw senses could focus on nothing but the pleasant scent of roses.

Slowly, like a symphony rising and swelling to its completion, Gabriel picked up an emotional vibration. It was desperation, and it flew at him like a frightened bird. The emotion became so powerful that he felt it as though it were his own.

Someone or something desperately wished him to keep him from leaving the house.

Over and over, the feeling burst forth with a clarity that was astonishing but frightening in its strength. The persistent buzzing grew louder, and he felt light-headed and weak.

The psychic experience lasted no more than a few seconds, but it seemed like an eternity. When it was over, he was dizzy. His eyes stung, his head throbbed, and his heart still pumped savagely. It took effort just to straighten and run a shaky hand over his face.

"Please don't go." The soft cadence of the feminine voice sounded far away and imagined, as the ocean sounded through a conch shell.

Holy Ghost of Christmas Present! The apparition had spoken to him. Excitement raced along his nerve endings. He stood perfectly still, hardly daring to breathe, willing it to speak again.

"Please, don't go."

How strange. The ghost had a familiar voice. Stranger still, he no longer felt its presence. No longer smelled the sweet rose fragrance.

Angie's name floated up through his mind like a sultry summer breeze. *Angie*. The epitome of feminine excitement. One part vixen, two parts angel. He smiled, a little dreamy, a little wistful.

"Are . . . you . . . all . . . right?"

Dull and dazed, he heard the question, though the voice seemed to be coming from a great distance.

"Gabe—Gabriel?"

His eyes widened as the fog began to lift from his mind. It *was* Angie, not a ghost, speaking to him. Pleasure mingled with professional disappointment. He let go of the doorknob and stared down at it, certain he was now hip-deep in something he couldn't as yet begin to fathom.

It took some effort, but he slowly turned to face Angie. Anxiety and some emotion he could not identify shimmered in her eyes. Her hands cupped her elbows, fingers nervously plucking at the sleeves of her tunic.

How long had she been standing in the arched passage between the foyer and dining room? Had she witnessed what had happened to him? Could she have felt the presence too?

"Are you all right?" she repeated, walking toward him.

He kept silent, not certain what would come out if he opened his mouth to speak.

"Sugar Booger, you bad cat," she scolded. "Stop that!" She bent down and detached the animal's claws from Gabriel's clothing. Holding the wiggling creature in her arms, she straightened. "I hope he didn't hurt you. I don't know what's gotten into him lately. He's never acted like this before."

Disappointment flooded through him again. She really had no idea that something extraordinary had just happened!

Gabriel badly wanted to share with her what he had experienced. But he knew it was best to keep it to himself, since he didn't have a shred of evidence to prove it. Without proof Angie wouldn't believe him. She would think he was crazy, or simply trying to con her.

"I'm fine," he finally managed to say. "Sugar Booger wasn't bothering me." He summoned a smile and, with some difficulty, maintained it. "I was just lost in thought for a moment, that's all."

"Oh." A look of relief replaced the anxiety in her eyes.

"Is there something more you wanted to say to me?

Or did you come to make sure I didn't pinch the sterling silver on my way out?"

He saw a flash of hurt pass over her delicate features, and he immediately regretted those last joking words. "I didn't mean that as a cheap shot, though I suppose it sounded like one. I'm sorry."

"No, don't apologize." She bowed her head, and his gaze locked on the golden halo of her hair. "I wouldn't blame you if you had meant it that way. It's no more than I deserve. I'm ashamed of the shabby way I've treated you."

He continued to stare at her hair. Her blatant honesty disarmed him, and he was speechless again.

Her fingers nervously stroked the cat's ears. "I made assumptions about you and your motives for coming here that *may* be unwarranted and unfair. Please forgive me."

Gabriel frowned, thinking he ought to stop her before she fell to her knees at his feet. What in creation had changed her attitude so drastically? Where was all this meek sincerity coming from?

When he remained silent, she went on, her voice faltering. "Of course, I wouldn't blame you if you couldn't find it in you to forget the way I've behaved."

She lifted her head and met his gaze. In her faint smile was a hint of the flirty and outrageous woman who had stirred up his libido. "My only excuse is that I can be a real bitch when I think the well-being and safety of the people I love is being threatened."

"Lucky people," he murmured, giving her a long and guarded look. Several uncomfortable emotions surfaced within him as he found himself wishing he were one of those people fortunate enough to be the center of Angie's fierce devotion. "My profession is an unusual one, so I understand why you would question my purpose in coming here. I just wish I could prove to you that I have no intention of harming your aunt, emotionally or financially."

"I'm beginning to believe that." Another smile touched her lips, a gentle one that enchanted him.

Lord, did she know what she did to him when her eyes went warm and she smiled like that? He wanted to lean forward and kiss her soft mouth. If he tried, though, she'd think he was a jerk or just plain out of his mind.

Absently, he reached up to pet the animal in her arms. His hand found the same spot upon its silky fur as Angie's. Their fingertips brushed, drew back as though shocked by an electrical current, then hesitantly met again.

Why wasn't she moving her hand away? Angie wondered. Her throat went dry as her body ignored the command of her brain. Her gaze traveled upward and locked with his. Such incredible eyes. Hypnotic eyes. If she wasn't very, very careful, she would fall under the spell of those beautiful eyes. On that uneasy thought, she lowered her gaze and moved her hand to encircle the cat's fat stomach.

"The day started out so ordinary." She laughed, feeling self-conscious again. "I prepared breakfast for my son and that nice honeymooning couple who left this morning. Miles and I bought school supplies." Her voice sounded odd to her, too breathless, too unsure. "I took Miles to Aunt Clover's house to play. I washed table linens and prepared to close the inn. If anyone had told me I would be inviting a ghostbuster to stay the night, I would have thought them insane." She looked up and smiled.

His hand stilled upon the cat's head. "*Are* you inviting me to stay?"

"Yes." She glanced away as heat flooded her cheeks. "But just for tonight," she added quickly. "I have to be honest: I'm still leery of this paranormal nonsense."

"Why?"

"I told you, I don't believe in it." A hint of irritation crept into her voice.

Smiling, he stopped rubbing the cat's ears. "I was asking why you're letting me stay."

She swallowed back the impulse to tell him it was because she loved with all her aching heart a little boy named Miles who reminded her of an unusual young boy called Gabriel; because she hadn't known until it had happened to her own child how deeply it could hurt to be mocked and excluded by one's peers; and because some small part of her wanted to give this man a chance to . . .

A chance to what? Her mouth twisted in a self-deprecating grimace. A chance to prove the purity of his motives? Or was it actually a chance for her to make up for past transgressions by making an effort to get to know Gabriel Richards, whom she had dismissed as a boy so many years ago? Or was it because some irrational part of her was attracted to the man the boy had become?

Life would be simpler, she thought, if she sent Gabriel back to Durham tonight. And if that nice smile of his didn't make his mouth look so tempting and sensual.

The drift of her thoughts dismayed her. She raised her chin and attempted a cool expression. "Call it guilt if you want."

"Guilt is a great motivator." His unfathomable eyes solemnly held her gaze. "But you don't strike me as a person who allows that emotion to influence her decisions."

"Just thank your lucky stars I'm not tossing you out of here on your butt," she said, feeling less sure of herself than she had a moment earlier. Dammit, she didn't want to analyze her reasons for letting him stay the night. "Get with the program, Gabriel. I'm making an attempt to be reasonable. Okay?"

He opened his mouth to correct her use of his name, then shut it quickly, realizing how ridiculous he'd sound. But oddly enough, he found he rather missed the easy, familiar way she'd shortened his name to Gabe.

"I'm offering you a bed for the night. Don't read too much into my motivation or the invitation."

He lowered his gaze before she could see how badly

he wished the bed she offered had been hers. When he glanced back up, his eyes locked on her full, soft lips. Once again, all he could think about was kissing that sultry, sassy mouth. Would she feel like satin and heat? Would she taste more sweet and tart than ripe summer strawberries, which were as red as her beautiful mouth? His heart began to thump hard against his chest, and his lungs fought for air.

"Take it or leave it."

He deliberately avoided her eyes for a moment as he struggled to curb the powerful physical impact of Angie Parker. He swore silently, then forced himself to speak in an even tone of voice, "That does sound quite reasonable. I'll take it. Thank you."

"Bring in whatever you need for the night. Tomorrow, we'll go see Ivy and straighten out this whole mess. And don't think I won't do my best to discourage Aunt Ivy from allowing you to hunt for her imaginary ghost."

He lifted his gaze to see her tightly hugging the disgruntled cat to her breasts like a shield. "And I hope you understand that I'm not backing off. I intend to persuade Mrs. Rule to go ahead with the investigation."

"I know that." She gave him a look almost as disgruntled as the cat's.

She started to walk away, then turned to face him. "You'll have to entertain yourself this evening. Don't expect me to cook for you, either."

He swallowed the laughter forming in his throat. "Can you cook?"

"Cooking is my life, sugar," she drawled in the purring, honeyed tone that teased Gabriel's senses so delightfully. "Men have been known to weep for joy at my dinner table."

Admiration spread through him as he watched her make a royal, head-held-high exit that wasn't ruined in the least by the sexy little sashay in her walk. He stayed where he was, watching the swinging of her loosely tied back hair, the provocative sway of her hips, her shimmering sexuality.

Now that was one hell of a woman. Sharing a bed with her would be a fascinating experience, he thought, breaking into what he feared was a sappy grin.

He swung around and tried the doorknob again. It turned easily.

He left the house and took a short walk around the property to absorb the impact of the psychic experience he'd had in the foyer. He was used to tuning in to the emotions of living human beings, but he'd never encountered the situation he now found himself in: tuning in to the emotions and presence of an entity. Why had he been able to *feel* the presence in the foyer? Why had he been able to tune in to the strong emotions it emanated?

When he could not come up with a logical explanation, he headed for his car. Tomorrow he would have to persuade Angie—with her aunt's help, he hoped—to allow him to investigate. No matter how long it took, he was determined to discover the source of the paranormal occurrences going on within the Kingston Inn.

❖ —————— ❖

"Hello?" The single word, spoken by a timid voice, sounded to Gabriel like a question rather than a greeting.

He hadn't heard anyone approach as he sifted through the luggage and equipment in the trunk of his car. He slung a garment bag over his shoulder and closed the trunk.

As he turned, he received another shock of familiarity. A few feet away stood the small boy he had seen in his dream.

The child's features, particularly his nose and eyes, were too large for his solemn, birdlike face. But someday, he thought, when the boy outgrew his extreme youth, those features would appear quite appealing. His fine blond hair was disheveled, unmanageable tufts sticking straight up as though he had either forgotten to comb it or was in the habit of running his fingers through it.

He had to be Angie's son. Behind thick glasses, his eyes were the same Nordic blue as hers. Instead of dreaminess, though, his gaze contained an adult directness that was at odds with his shy voice and manner.

"Hello." Gabriel smiled. "Are you a karate student?" He glanced over the boy's kimono-style shirt and matching white trousers, which hung loosely on the child's thin frame.

"No, sir. I study aikido." The keenness in the eyes behind the black-rimmed spectacles gave Gabriel the distinct impression he was being weighed, measured, and neatly dissected. "I find the personal philosophy of aikido infinitely more satisfying than most other forms of martial arts."

Interest flickered through Gabriel at the formality and maturity of the child's speech. "I have a friend who would concur wholeheartedly with that statement. He teaches aikido in Raleigh."

"Is your friend a master?" The boy came forward slowly, clutching a canvas bag, the laces of one black high-top sneaker trailing along the ground.

"Yes, but he modestly contends he is merely a student."

Nodding with approval, the boy stopped within an arm's length of Gabriel. "Jake says no matter how proficient we become in something, we're still lifelong students."

"A wise man. Is he your aikido master?"

"Yes, sir. He's also my best friend and family by choice. That's what my mother calls people who aren't related to us but whom we love like family anyway."

A sudden smile made the child's plain face appear radiantly angelic. Gabriel's mouth curved into an unconscious smile in response. "Jake married my godmother Nila last year. I'm going to be their baby's godfather, when it is born," he said confidentially. "I think I shall like that very much."

He lifted one frail-looking hand to be shaken, and it all but disappeared into Gabriel's larger one. "I'm Miles

Parker. I'm very happy to make your acquaintance, Dr. Richards."

"You know who I am?" Gabriel asked blankly.

"Of course. I recognize you from the photograph that accompanied the article you wrote on what separates the normal from the paranormal." Miles readjusted the glasses on his long, straight nose. "I found you for Aunt Ivy, you know."

"You *found* me for Mrs. Rule?" Did he sound as bewildered as he felt?

"Yes, sir. When Aunt Ivy and I realized we needed an expert in evaluating paranormal experiences to advise us, I contacted two psychic research organizations, both of which highly recommended you. Then I read everything you've published in scientific journals. I was *particularly* impressed by the way you exposed that phony poltergeist two years ago."

Gabriel was momentarily taken aback. His initial assessment of the boy's intelligence shot upward. Miles Parker wasn't just bright, he was extraordinary. "How resourceful of you," he said without perceptible hesitation.

"Thank you. Have you just arrived?"

"No, I've been here for a while."

"You've met my mother?" Miles worried his hair into a few more peaks with his fingers.

"I have."

"Then she doesn't object to the project?" he asked, eyes brightening.

"Unfortunately, she does object." Gabriel knew there was no use in offering false comfort. "She has only agreed to allow me to stay the night and to discuss the situation with Mrs. Rule in the morning."

Miles stubbed at the gravel with the toe of one sneaker. "I was afraid of that. Mama is dead set against anything supernatural, you see. That's why we kept our plans from her." He sighed, then fixed his ardent gaze upon Gabriel's face. "I know it was wrong of us to do that, but we must help the poor Shadow Lady. You *can* help her, can't you?"

Gabriel didn't have the slightest idea if he could or not. In fact, if Angie had her way, he wasn't certain he would even get a chance to try. But he found himself unable to resist the pleading look in the eyes raised so hopefully to his. "That's a tough question, Miles. I honestly can't promise results, but I will try."

Apparently, that was enough for the boy. He squared his shoulders and fell into step with Gabriel as they walked toward the house.

"Spiders are a *particular* interest of mine," he said. "Do you happen to know anything about the subject, sir?"

Gabriel admitted he was somewhat knowledgeable on arachnid and was rewarded with a look that bordered on hero worship.

Miles immediately began to point out several wide, flat, sheetlike webs spun by grass spiders. "I found a *particularly* beautiful orb web created by a common orange garden spider in the shrubs in the side yard. I'll show it to you later, if you like."

"I'd like that very much," he responded, smiling down at the eager boy who reminded him of himself at the same age.

By the time they entered the house, Gabriel felt he understood the source of the guilt that had led Angie to invite him to stay the night.

FOUR

It was nearly ten o'clock. The events of the day were rapidly fading in their importance to Gabriel, and he was feeling relaxed. He sat straddling a kitchen chair, one forearm resting on its back, a glass of chilled white wine in his hand, and an admiring eye on Angie.

In the hours that had passed she had been friendly but reserved. She and her son had given him the grand tour of the house, then they'd dined on take-out pizza and stimulating conversation. Afterward he'd enjoyed a challenging game of chess with Miles. Angie had sat nearby, working on a complicated needlepoint design.

After putting her son to bed, she'd disappeared into the kitchen. He'd wandered in a few minutes later to find her wearing an apron with *Kiss the Cook* imprinted across the front.

As he sat watching her whip up a batch of brownies, Gabriel decided he'd like nothing better than kissing this particular cook. Okay, so there was one thing he'd like even better than kissing her. Unfortunately, the sexy lady had weathered enough shocks, and he didn't think she'd stand—or lie down—for either of those things.

It had been a rough day for Angie, he thought, feeling a wave of sympathy for her. She'd barely had time to come to terms with him, both present and past, when her son had revealed to her his part in finding a parapsychologist. During dinner, she'd sustained yet another shock: Miles had confessed that he had seen the Shadow Lady.

According to the boy, the apparition often sat beside his bed in a chair that materialized with her. Miles had claimed that the Shadow Lady watched over him while he slept. Angie had looked as though she didn't know whether to laugh or immediately haul the kid off to a psychiatrist.

"The ghost brings her own furniture?" she'd asked her son, and Gabriel had found himself hard pressed not to laugh at her astounded expression.

To her credit, she had quickly recovered from both startling revelations from her son. Gabriel was impressed by the caring but firm parental manner in which she'd dealt with Miles.

She was quite a lady. Her emotions were tied up in knots, but she could still smile.

He took a sip of his wine without taking his eyes off Angie. He supposed it wasn't very charitable to hope she didn't have a special man in her life, but that's how he felt.

Angie was doing what she often did when she had something to worry about: She cooked. Since she had a truckload of things to worry about, she was making rocky road brownies.

The cooking and worrying about Ivy and Miles, however, didn't totally keep her mind off one troublesome ghostbuster. She was constantly aware of Gabriel as a man, and she really wished he hadn't come into the kitchen. She could feel his eyes tracking her movements. Every time she glanced his way, she felt attraction flow through her like a warm stream.

She sneaked another peak at him. After she'd given him a tour of the house that afternoon and assigned him a bedroom upstairs, he'd changed clothes. He didn't look anything like a stuffy businessman now; he looked casual and good, in jeans and a red plaid shirt with the sleeves rolled up. Too good.

If only he weren't a ghostbuster.

Stop with the "if only's," she told herself as she poured the brownie mixture into a baking dish. She carried it over to the oven and thumped the dish inside.

"Your son is a great kid," Gabriel said behind her. "Very bright and well behaved."

"Thank you." She turned to face him. "He is a very good child—most of the time." Her laugh was helpless, short. "It blows my mind every time I think about him conspiring with Ivy to get you here without me finding out."

"We *need* Dr. Richards," Miles had told her in that

solemn, adult manner of his when she'd tucked him in bed. "He can help the Shadow Lady, Mama. I *know* he can."

Angie sighed heavily. She picked up the glass of wine she'd poured herself and left on the counter while preparing the brownies.

"Are you worried about your son?"

"I worry about everyone in my family. But Miles is my most pressing concern," she said, then wondered why she'd told him something so personal.

She walked toward the table, and as she seated herself, Gabriel got up to turn his chair around.

"Have you no concern for yourself?" he asked.

"For myself?" she said, wrinkling her brow. "There's really no need for that."

"Perhaps I should have said, any *thought* for yourself. Your thoughts and concerns seem to center on needs of family and friends. But what about *you*? What do you want for yourself?"

She looked at him for a long moment. "Nothing really. I have everything I want or need." A dismissive shrug of her shoulders made the wide neck of her tunic slip down on one side. She saw his gaze fix on her bare shoulder, and a tingling sensation raced over her skin, as if he'd actually touched her. She slid the tunic back into place, acknowledging to herself that the sexual attraction she'd felt toward him earlier hadn't faded one bit.

He lifted his gaze back to her face, his rueful smile telling her he was sorry she'd spoiled his view. "Surely there's something more you want out of life for yourself?" he asked.

She frowned at his question. Maybe it was because she was tired of being thought of as a merry and not too bright widow with too much money and too much time on her hands, maybe she was reaching some turning point in her life, but whatever the reason, she threw caution to the winds and told him the whole truth.

"You mean more out of life than being a semi-idle widow? You think I ought to be harboring some great ambition to do something more useful with my life than raising a child, cooking, cleaning, and puttering around my friend's store?"

She paused for breath. "Well, Gabe, the shocking truth is that I don't have any burning ambition. I *like* being a mother. I like being there for my kid when he gets home from school. This fluff-brained bunny gets a kick out of creating a new recipe and making Halloween costumes. I'm happy being a caretaker. Creating a secure haven where my family knows they are loved, no matter how rotten the outside world treats them, is what I do best."

She stopped talking, shocked at herself, and took a big gulp of her wine. "Sorry, I didn't mean to jump on my soapbox."

Gabriel reached over and removed the glass she was rolling between her palms. Then he leaned forward and lifted her hand to his lips for a brief kiss.

She laughed. "What was that for?"

"For being so passionate about what you do." He smiled and continued in a softer voice. "It was your hopes and dreams I was inquiring about, not justification for the role you've chosen in life."

"Oh." She flushed with embarrassment.

Her hopes and dreams were simple ones. All she really wanted was to love and be loved. She couldn't tell him that. It was too personal. Too private. He might laugh.

"I know it isn't easy raising an exceptional child," he said, changing the subject as though he'd picked up on her discomfort.

Gabriel was as nice as he was handsome, she thought. But she was old enough—and, she hoped, wise enough—not to let her hormones or emotions get control where a man was concerned. Friendly but a bit reserved—that was the best attitude to strike.

"No, it isn't easy. Nor is it easy *being* an exceptional child." She smiled quickly, apologetically. "But you know that from experience."

"The early years are the roughest." Gabriel didn't like talking about his childhood. Far too much of it had been painful and sometimes harrowing. But he could see that she needed to talk to someone who knew what both she and Miles were going through.

"My parents had set ideas about what a *normal* childhood should be," he told her. "I wasn't a typical kid, though. I didn't fit into the normal life they wanted to provide for me. Once they stopped fighting the obvious, all three of us were a lot happier."

"What do you mean they 'stopped fighting the obvious'?" she asked, swirling the wine around in her glass and staring at the vortex.

"They sent me to a school for gifted children and teens in Durham."

"Alone?" She glanced up, looking appalled. "To a boarding school? How old were you?"

"Thirteen."

"That was the year after you moved away from Danville?"

He nodded. "It was the best thing they could have done for me. My life improved a hundred percent the two years I was there."

He watched her stare thoughtfully into her glass again. In all his twenty-eight years, he'd never felt such a deep hunger for a woman. He hadn't known he was starving for that kind of primal attraction until today. Until he'd met Angie again. For a second he allowed himself to drink in her nearness, her scent. She smelled like heaven and warm summer nights.

"May I ask you something?" She looked up at him and seemed to try so hard to smile, her lips trembled slightly. "If it's too personal, just tell me to buzz off."

"Ask me anything you want."

"Were you happy at that school? Did you—did you feel as though you fit in? Socially, I mean."

His smile showed her he understood. "Yes, I was happy there. For the first time I didn't feel so different or alienated. I was with kids who were just like me."

Just like him, in all respects save one. But that one difference hadn't seemed so great in that setting. "That's where I finally began to accept myself for who and what I was."

Keeping his tone very casual, he asked, "Have you considered that option for Miles?"

She looked at him for a long moment, saying nothing, as though she were having second thoughts about opening up and trusting him. That bothered him.

"Look, pretty lady." He touched the back of her hand. "I don't mean to pry. But I like Miles."

She smiled ruefully, and he could easily guess what she was worried about. Miles seemed to have taken to him, as though he had instantly recognized in Gabriel a kindred spirit. Angie, however, still suspected that his motives for being there were not entirely on the up-and-up. If that were the case, her aunt *and* her son would be hurt.

He could see tension seeping into her body and knew her emotional temperature was rising. He wished she didn't feel as though she had to be so cautious around him. Wisely, though, he kept silent, waiting for her to sort through her thoughts and speak first.

"Miles was declared mentally gifted at age three." She got up and paced to look out the window above the sink. "Educators and counselors have urged me to consider sending him to a school for the gifted."

She turned, lifted her hands, then let them fall. "But he's so young. I can't bear the thought of him living alone among strangers who won't love him like I do. He *needs* me."

Gabriel crossed the room to stand near her. "Of course he needs you." He reached up to tuck her hair behind her ear.

His tender gesture and warm smile set off a sensual fluttering deep inside Angie. She dismissed her reaction as normal and healthy, telling herself that any woman would find Gabriel Richards attractive.

"I know it's not my place to tell you how to raise your son," he continued. "But Miles also has a brilliant mind that needs to be nurtured. Fourth-grade work isn't going to be much of a challenge for a kid who is more knowledgeable in many subjects than some adult scholars."

"My son is doing fine." She started to move away.

He caught her by the elbow, sliding his fingers down the length of her arm to capture her hand.

"Is he?" His gaze held hers as firmly as he held her hand. "Or do you just want to think so?"

Honesty forced her to admit privately, even though it hurt, that Gabriel was right. But it didn't make it any easier to swallow.

"I'm not stupid, Gabe. If you must know, I do plan to move closer to a gifted school for him. But not in the immediate future."

He didn't respond to that, and she saw that his attention had strayed. His gaze swept over her face, returning again and again to her mouth in a way that told her he was hot and hungry for a taste of her. He was stealing her breath and making her feel as though she were being run through a sexual wringer.

It wasn't a bad feeling. Far from it. She was enjoying it too much for her own good.

Even though she was finding Gabriel very likable and—Lord have mercy!—*very* desirable, she could not blithely dismiss her concerns about him. What if his motives for being there weren't as academic as he claimed?

Before she started liking him too much, she decided, she'd better find out if he really was what he claimed to be. Her friend Nila's husband, Jake, could discreetly check into his background for her. Though he was retired from the Drug Enforcement Administration, Jake still had contacts within law enforcement agencies all over the country.

Gabriel regarded Angie with astonishment. He'd heard her thoughts in his mind as clearly as if she'd spoken them aloud. It was the first time he'd ever experienced telepathic communication. Until now, his talent had been limited to an erratic ability to read emotional emanations and to the acquisition, without sensory mediation, of information about a place, event, or object.

He set aside that fascinating aberration and considered what he'd "heard" mentally. He supposed he ought to be offended that she was going to have him checked out, but he wasn't. Her concern was based on her love for her aunt and son. He certainly couldn't fault her for that.

Angie was growing uneasy with the silence, as well as with her physical reaction to his nearness. "Why are you holding my hand?" she demanded unsteadily.

"Because I like touching you." His thumb moved lightly over her knuckles, sending paralyzing currents of excitement throughout her. "Holding hands with you was one of my fondest ninth-grade fantasies. If you don't like it, I'll stop."

A flush crept up from her throat to her cheeks. She ought to say she didn't like it at all. But she couldn't, because her fingers were disobeying her mind by entwining with his.

His expression suddenly altered from desire to something she couldn't read. "I realize you don't want to deal with it, Angie, but your aunt and your son are convinced something paranormal is going on in this house. They even claim they've seen this Shadow Lady. Let me stay and find out if it's true. What harm could it do?"

It could cause a lot of harm, she thought. She desired this man, and she hadn't felt that emotion for a very long time.

"I don't want to discuss it." She jerked her hand from his and brushed past him.

He followed her and stood close as she opened the oven to peek at the brownies. "You can't ignore the possibility, pretty lady."

"Sure I can."

The rich chocolate confection looked done to her. She opened a drawer and took out two badly crocheted pot holders Clover had made for her sister last Christmas. Angie had received two that were almost identical, except hers were a horrible lime green and red instead of purple and fuchsia.

"I suppose you think you can also ignore the chemistry between us?"

Angie resisted the temptation to throw the pan of brownies at him. "Chemistry? That's ridiculous."

"Is it?"

Her body responded instantly to the undisguised desire she saw in his eyes. Need struggled with common sense. The latter won out, but only by a very small margin. It would be foolish, she knew, to risk accepting him at Boy Scout face value.

"Don't get pushy, Gabe." She managed a cool stare before plunking the baking dish down on the stove top.

"Angie—"

"Forget it, Gabe. I refuse to be drawn into a debate on ghosts and chemistry." She turned her back on him and headed to the table.

He trailed after her, laughing. It was a very pleasant sound, one she knew she could easily get used to hearing.

"I was only going to ask if you're dating anyone. Seriously, I mean."

She glanced at him. "No." Without her permission her lips formed a tiny smile.

"Neither am I."

She wiped the smile off her face. "Is your room satisfactory?"

"It's charming."

"Good night. I hope you sleep well." She picked up the wineglasses.

"Was that a hint that I should go to my room?"

She nodded as she passed him on her way to the sink. He followed her again, making her think of a persistent puppy nipping at her heels.

"Without dessert?" The pitiful tone of his voice didn't match the mischief in his eyes.

She grabbed a knife, cut into the hot brownies, and dumped a generous helping onto a napkin. "Here. Take it with you."

"Thanks," he said, managing to caress the back of her hand as he took the treat from her. He was grinning as he turned to leave.

One night, Angie thought, filling the sink with water to wash the mixing bowl and utensils. Tomorrow he'd be gone and life could return to normal. Somehow that didn't appeal to her as much as it should have.

"It's okay with me," she heard him call from across the room.

"What's okay?" She squeezed drops of lemony-smelling detergent into the water.

"I don't mind if you want to ask your friend Jake to check into my background."

A chill raced up her spine. She dropped the plastic bottle of dishwashing liquid. Water splashed over the bib of her apron.

Slowly she pivoted to face him. She stared at him for a long moment as she steadied herself.

"How did you know?" she whispered.

His gaze locked with hers as he walked back across the room. He stopped in front of her.

"Don't look so scared," he said, lifting one hand to her cheek. "I told you I'm clairvoyant."

She was too startled to be embarrassed that he knew what she was planning to do.

"Thanks for the brownie."

"You're welcome." Her voice quivered.

She could swear his eyes grew more mysterious, more seductive, as his fingers trailed down the side of her face. "I know why men weep for joy at your dinner table. It has nothing to do with your culinary talents." His voice, low and husky, produced a weakness behind her knees. "Good night, beautiful lady."

Wrapping her arms around her middle to quell the fluttering inside, she watched Gabriel walk away.

For a woman who didn't relish complications, she realized her life was suddenly overflowing with them.

Gabriel slept fitfully. He kept waking to the creaks and groans of an unfamiliar house, to a hard rain peppering the windowpanes, and to the feel of a mattress that was not his own. Once he even thought he heard the sound of someone playing the piano. When he came fully awake, though, the touchingly sweet music was gone.

Sometime later, he heard the cat clawing to get in. He reluctantly got up. When he opened the door, he saw the feline arch its back as it stared down the dark hallway toward the stairwell. It hissed like a broken radiator, then scrambled inside the bedroom.

Gabriel stepped out into the hall, straining to see into every shadow, nook, and cranny. He didn't see or hear anything out of the ordinary.

As he started back into the room, he caught a faint scent of rose water. It was the same smell he'd picked up in the foyer that afternoon. He stood perfectly still, waiting and hoping to feel the entity's presence as he had before.

Nothing happened. The scent grew weaker and weaker, until he was left wondering if it had really been there at all.

The scientist in him was frustrated as he went back to bed. He regretted not pushing Angie harder to allow him to set up the infrared camera and sensitive recording equipment he needed to confirm the entity's physical presence. Without that confirmation, he was left to wonder if the equipment would have recorded anything in the form of sight, heat, and field magnetic changes.

Sugar Booger poked his head out from under the bed as Gabriel approached. He grudgingly picked the animal up and set him down at the end of the bed.

As Gabriel crawled back under the covers, he heard a clock chime three times somewhere in the house.

❧ ———————— ❧

As the clock struck three, a single tear slid down Julia's magnolia-white cheek.

Over her shoulder, she cast one last lingering look down the hallway to the closed door of the one she prayed could save her. Then she began her descent, slowly and resolutely, down the stairs.

Hope shone in her eyes for the first time in over a hundred years.

FIVE

The next morning Gabriel showered, dressed, picked up the cat, and eagerly followed his nose downstairs. The aroma of coffee and the yeasty smell of something good baking in the oven drew him to the kitchen.

He found Angie sitting at the table, her chin propped in one palm, a cup of coffee in front of her. She was staring at the wall, looking almost meditative. He didn't think it was a peaceful meditation, because the ashtray beside her contained several cigarette butts, as well as a lit one.

The table was set for three with china, linen napkins, a plate of fresh fruit, and a glass pitcher of orange juice. He noticed that two of the place settings had already been used, and he found himself somewhat disappointed that she and Miles had obviously dined without him.

She glanced up as he approached. "Good morning."

"Good morning."

She frowned at him. "Where did you find Sugar Booger? Miles has been searching the house for him."

"Oh, sorry about that." Gabriel put the animal down and it headed straight for its bowl of food. "He scratched on my door last night and I let him in."

"That's odd." She looked puzzled. "Sugar Booger hasn't willingly gone upstairs since the day we got here."

"He must feel safe with me for some reason."

"Maybe." She didn't sound convinced. "Are you hungry?"

"Starved. Is that cinnamon I smell?"

"Uh-huh. Cinnamon rolls. Homemade."

"If they're half as good as the brownies you made last night, I could eat a dozen."

Angie extinguished her cigarette, realizing she'd already reached the limit of three a day she'd set for herself. Darn it. It was partly his fault.

During the night, she'd convinced herself that her physical response to Gabriel was nothing more than a fluke. But from the quickening of her heart rate the minute he'd entered the kitchen, she knew she'd only been fooling herself.

Her gaze flickered over him. He was dressed in gray slacks and a white shirt that was open at the neck. Draped over his arm was a lightweight tweed blazer with suede patches at the elbows. His hair was still damp from the shower, one lone wave errantly trailing over his brow.

"Sit down." She motioned to the chair across from her.

His smile was warm but not ingratiating. It told her he would understand if she didn't want to smile back. She did anyway.

Gabriel draped his jacket over one chair, then pulled out another and sat down. He helped himself to the sliced cantaloupe and strawberries, while his gaze traveled over Angie as she got up and walked across the room.

Angie elevated feminine clothing to an art form. A pleated navy miniskirt with a side split did a good job of letting his appreciative eyes catch a polite but provocative glimpse of her slender, beautifully formed thigh. A white knit blouse outlined her perfect breasts and hinted at the nipples beneath. Cinching her small waist was a big brass belt of linked gold chains. Whenever she turned sideways, the allure of her lean silhouette was enough to make him forget all about homemade cinnamon rolls.

His gaze shimmied down her bare legs to her feet as she walked back to the table, a coffeepot in her hand. He found himself fascinated by each well-shaped foot and each pedicured, red-polished toenail.

How bizarre that he should get such a thrill out of looking at a woman's feet. Either he was developing a latent foot fetish or he was falling in love. He opted for the latter, because he didn't like the thought of turning into a pervert at this stage of his young life.

He met her gaze and said the first thing that came to mind. "I like that outfit. You look very pretty."

"Thank you." She filled his cup with coffee.

"Next to you, I look like a nice old professor who hasn't seen the inside of a men's clothing shop in years."

She followed his gaze to the jacket he'd placed on the chair next to him. "I like nice guys and old professors."

"You do?"

"My late husband was a professor at Georgetown University," she explained as she refilled her own cup. "Jon was a nice guy. He was also forty years older than me."

She went around the table and smoothed her free hand over the blazer's nubby weave. "His favorite sports coat was very similar to this one." She smiled fondly. "It was threadbare in places, though, and he'd worn a hole in one of the suede patches. The only time I ever saw Jon pitch a fit and pout was when I threw that old rag away. He dug it right back out of the trash can."

She laughed softly as she set the coffeepot on a warming tray on the table. "Every summer, Jon worked for one of the government think tanks, and he simply couldn't go without that garment. He called it his 'thinking coat.'"

Gabriel whistled silently. Jon Parker must have been a certified genius in his field. The government employed only the cream of the intellectual crop in its civilian and military think tanks.

His thoughtful gaze trailed after her as she crossed the kitchen to check on the rolls in the oven. "If anyone had asked me whatever became of the vibrant butterfly girl I'd known in high school, I would have said she probably married one of the jocks that always hung around her."

That made her laugh. "If asked the same question about you, I would have said you probably went on to be a rocket scientist. Life is certainly full of interesting little twists, isn't it?"

"You can say that again." Never in his wildest imagination would he have imagined the "Geek" would ever be sitting at the table of the "Beauty," about to chow down on cinnamon rolls she'd made with her own two hands.

"Were you a student at Georgetown when you met him?" he asked.

"No. I had just graduated from Georgia State." She took a pan from the oven and set it on the stove top. "I met Jon when I was interviewing for a job at the National Gallery of Art." The gold bracelets adorning her arm jangled as she transferred the rolls to the plate.

"How did you meet him?"

"I was sitting in one of the galleries that displays some of my favorite nineteenth-century paintings. I was feeling sorry for myself and trying not to cry." She glanced over her shoulder and smiled wryly. "I'd just discovered that a degree in art history alone didn't mean diddle. The Gallery director wanted someone with experience, or at least a master's degree.

"Anyway, Jon happened to be visiting the Gallery

that day. He came over, sat down beside me, and handed me his handkerchief without saying a word. After I'd cried and sniffled for a while . . ." Her voice trailed off as though she were momentarily lost in the memory, then she continued in a softer tone. "He looked at me and smiled. He wasn't a handsome man, but when he smiled he was beautiful. 'The heart,' he said to me, 'has its reasons which Reason does not know.' "

He'd never known the real Angie Sinclair, Gabriel suddenly realized. When they were kids, he had been just as guilty as she of not looking beyond the surface. As a boy, he'd been wrapped up in his own problems, unable to see more than a few glimpses of what lay beneath the Beauty's lovely face. He'd viewed her as the perfect golden girl, loved and accepted by all. In his immaturity, he'd thought that a girl like her couldn't possibly ever have problems of her own, couldn't possibly ever have a reason to cry or fail to get what she wanted.

That look at his own preconceived notions about her made him feel a bit humble.

"Emotion against intellect," he said, thinking about what Jon Parker had first said to her. "Isn't that the French sentiment that more or less spawned the romantic movement in art?"

"I'm impressed, Gabe. You know your art history."

"Art Appreciation 101." He grinned sheepishly. "What I know about art or its history could fit on the head of a pin, with room to spare."

She smiled at him as she dumped the spatula she'd been using into the sink. "I like a man who's brave enough to admit he doesn't know everything."

"I've even been known to stop and ask for directions when I'm lost."

She laughed. He took as much pleasure in her laughter as he did in her form and grace, the excellent flavor of her coffee, and the homey smells filling her kitchen.

"What happened after that?" he prompted.

"We talked for hours. It's strange really. We didn't have much in common, except for a love of nineteenth-century paintings. But I remember feeling as though in Jon I'd suddenly found the other half of myself. We were married two weeks later. So I got the job I really wanted after all."

"At the National Gallery?"

"No. Being a wife. I told you, I wasn't born with burning ambition in my soul."

Angie usually didn't care what people thought of her. The truth was she deliberately fostered her flighty image as a way of threshing the golden wheat from the chaff. Anyone worth knowing would take the trouble to delve deeper.

With Gabriel, though, both last night and this morning, she felt compelled to open up and show him a little of what she was inside. "All I ever wanted to do was make a home and raise a family with someone I loved with all my heart and soul and who loved me in return. With Jon

I was lucky enough to have it all. He made me feel I was of value simply because I existed."

"I think he was the fortunate one." Gabriel's voice was a husky rasp. A fierce hunger in his eyes, made all the more intense by his wistful smile, caused a shiver of sensual awareness to work its way up her spine.

Her brain filled with a jumble of thoughts and feelings, she turned away to gaze out the window. A part of her wanted to accept the flare of warmth spreading through her veins; another part didn't trust herself to keep things in perspective.

"How long were you married?" he asked, reclaiming her attention.

"Three of the best years of my life." She picked up the plate and walked over to the table.

As she served him two rolls, it suddenly occurred to her that the cold, hard knot of grief she usually felt when talking about her husband hadn't been there when she'd spoken to Gabriel just now. In a strange way, she felt bereft, because that grief had been a part of her for so long. Yet she also felt lighter, freer.

A chapter in her life had just ended, she thought in blinding amazement. The memory of her husband and their special time together would linger on in her heart, but she would no longer grieve for what was lost, no longer hurt for what couldn't be.

In that odd moment, she finally kissed her cherished memories good-bye and closed the book on their love story. She was no longer Jon's widow. She was just herself. Angie Sinclair Parker, a woman who looked forward to the future, a woman who was free to give her heart to whomever she pleased.

Gabriel sat still, staring up at her. He sensed something very significant had just occurred inside Angie's head. An image popped into his mind, one of shackles being broken. It frustrated him that he had no idea what it meant.

For a second, he wished he could pick up on her thoughts as he had last night. Then he reminded himself that was not only a selfish wish, but an invasion of privacy as well. He could feel her emotions, though, rising like a helium-filled balloon in an uplifting air current . . . joy, happiness, freedom. That was more than he had any right to know.

She seemed to float back to earth, then gave him a startled glance as though she'd forgotten he was there. "You're not eating," she said with a tiny frown. "Don't you like cinnamon rolls?"

"I'm nuts about 'em." He took the plate she was holding and set it on the table. "Will you keep me company while I eat?"

Smiling rather shyly, she pulled out her chair and seated herself. "Did you sleep well?"

He didn't want to be rude and say no. "Yes, thank you." He accompanied the lie with a great big smile. "The music woke me up once, though."

She frowned again. "I beg your pardon?"

"You play very well," he said, picking up his fork to

cut into one of the warm, fragrant rolls. "Are you in the habit of getting up in the middle of the night to play the piano?"

"Is that supposed to be a joke? Do you think that amuses me, Gabriel Richards? Do you see me smiling? Am I laughing?"

He thought she was being a mite melodramatic over a straightforward question. "All I asked is if you had a habit of getting up in the middle of the night to play the piano."

Her expression darkened. Her eyes flashed like lightning. She looked as though she might snatch back his cinnamon rolls.

He curled his arm around the plate, just in case. Cinnamon rolls hot from the oven were a particular weakness of his, and he wasn't giving these babies up without a fight.

"Get yourself a clown suit and a big red nose," she said, "then a person would know when you're joking." She put her hands on her hips. "You know very well there isn't a piano anywhere in this house."

His eyes widened, and he almost choked on his excitement and a rather large bite of roll. Grabbing his glass of orange juice, he washed them both down.

"Weren't you paying attention on the tour I gave you yesterday?"

He shook his head and grinned happily. There could have been a dozen musical instruments in the house, for all he remembered. His mind had been on other things: his psychic experience in the foyer, Miles, the provocative wiggle in Angie's walk.

"I thought not," she said in an exasperated voice. "Now what's all this nonsense about hearing me play the piano?"

"I distinctly heard piano music last night." Wanting to rule out all probable possibilities before gladly reaching the improbable one, he asked, "Do you or Miles sleep with a radio on?"

She picked up the coffeepot. Gabriel quickly held out his cup, because she looked like she was thinking of pouring the hot liquid over his head. She didn't, which relieved him greatly.

"No, we do not," she said. Her eyes narrowed and she shook her finger at him. "I know what you're thinking. Don't even try suggesting the ghost *materialized* a piano out of nothing. I don't buy it. If you heard music last night, you heard it in your dreams."

"Angie, I know what I heard."

"Bull dooty. And that's my final two words on the subject. Eat your breakfast, Gabe. The sooner we see my aunt, the sooner you'll be back on the road to Durham."

At least, Angie hoped so. Ivy could be very stubborn when she put her mind to it. Unless Jake had dug up something shady about Gabriel, Angie didn't think she had a prayer of persuading her aunt to drop the ghost-hunt craziness.

Gabriel put his hand on her wrist to stop her as she pushed back her chair. "Your friend Jake is meeting us at the nursing facility. You're hoping he's found something about me that will help you persuade Mrs. Rule to drop the investigation."

Angie could no more have held back her gasp of surprise than she could control her awareness of the heat of his skin. Seconds ticked by as she eyed him warily.

He hadn't read her mind *again*, she rationalized. It was impossible. The night before she'd managed to explain to herself how Gabriel had *seemed* to know what she was thinking. She knew Miles had told Gabriel about Jake, his friend and aikido master. So wasn't it reasonable to assume that Miles might have mentioned Jake's former occupation as a DEA agent? Knowing that, it would have been easy for Gabriel to guess that she might ask him for help.

She wanted very badly to believe that. Still, she couldn't stop the doubts from seeping into her mind. Especially since he was right again: Jake and Nila were meeting her at the nursing facility.

She shifted uneasily, then raised her chin and dredged up a bright smile as she broke free of his hold on her wrist. "Congratulations. You got lucky and guessed correctly."

Gabriel regarded her closely. She'd spoken in an even voice. But something in her tone, in her eyes, told him she wasn't quite as certain about that as she wanted him to think.

"Don't frown so," he murmured, leaning across the

table to put his palm against her cheek. "Everything will work out okay."

"I think—" she began, but her voice broke and she had to try again. "I think you scare me, Gabriel Richards." Her words came out in a rush.

"Why?" He let his hand slide down to her shoulder. Beneath his fingers, her muscles were knotted with tension.

"Because I like to keep things simple. You're a complication I don't need."

"Life is dull without a few well-chosen complications." He got up and went to stand behind her, then gently began working on the knots in her shoulder muscles.

"Gabe—"

"Relax," he ordered softly, stroking away her tension, enjoying the warmth and resilience of her. "You worry too much."

"My aunt and my son swear they've seen a ghost. You can read my mind. And you . . ."

She lifted her hand to cover his as he started massaging her neck. "You make me feel things I haven't felt in a very long time."

Gabriel drew a breath, savoring the scent and softness of her skin and enjoying the spark of desire her words generated in him. "The feeling is mutual. You make me feel things I've *never* felt before."

"I'm not sure I like this." She slipped out of the chair and stood facing him, staring in paralyzed, fascinated silence.

"I don't think that's true. You just don't know what to do with it—I mean, me." He made a slow assessment of her face, his gaze roaming over her delicate features and ever-widening eyes. Without thinking, he snaked out an arm and captured her around the waist, drawing her closer. Before he realized his own intentions, he was bending his head and kissing her.

Angie was too surprised to move. Then she was too busy savoring the richness of his kiss. It had begun tentatively, as though his actions had startled him as much as they had her. But it had quickly gathered momentum.

She raised up on tiptoe and her arms met behind his neck. His mouth took possession of her half-parted lips, and he slid his tongue inside for delectable exploration. Deep, swirling sensations spread languor throughout her, in direct opposition to the racing of her heartbeat. She felt dizzy and weightless as their breaths mingled in a long, slow kiss.

Gabriel's hands spread across her back and moved down her spine, feeling her warmth through the thin fabric of her blouse. Sensations of intimacy spread a warm lassitude through his lower limbs. He was aware of a driving need for her, hot and insatiable.

He didn't want to let her go. The feelings she aroused in him were so erotic, it was a miracle he could still stand.

He broke the kiss and gave her an extra-long hug, then let her go. That was difficult. She fit well. Too well.

His gaze locked with hers. Seconds went by in an

electrified silence. He counted every one of them as a thousand thoughts crossed his mind: how beautiful she was, how she could become an obsession, how he couldn't escape the heart-bursting feeling that his fate was irrevocably tied up with hers.

Angie couldn't imagine what he thought of her now. She'd responded to his kiss as though starved for that kind of affection. Which, she realized, she was. But not from just any man. *From him.*

He smiled at her and with the knuckle of one finger gently stroked under her chin. "Is it bad, what I did? Do I owe you an apology?"

"If you mean kissing me . . ." She laughed and wondered why she should feel so self-conscious. "It wasn't bad at all." In fact, it had just about curled her toes, brief though it had been. But she wasn't going to encourage him by telling him that. "No apology necessary."

"I'm glad." He touched her face in a gesture that seemed almost reverent. "It would make me feel hypocritical to apologize for something I enjoyed so much. Did I mention I've always had a crush on you?"

"I . . . We're not kids anymore, Gabe."

"No. We're not." He spoke so softly that the words seemed to caress the small distance between them in the same way that his fingertips were now caressing her jaw.

She drew a single, sharp breath, her shoulders quite still, almost rigid. It had been so long since a man had touched her with such . . . tenderness.

"Angie—"

"It's getting late," she said quickly. "I have to take Miles to the baby-sitter before we . . . leave for the hospital."

She spun away and practically ran from the room, sending the cat scattering before her.

Forty-five minutes later, Gabriel wondered if he was ever going to see Mrs. Rule. Angie had barely spoken a civil word to him since she'd come back from taking her son to the baby-sitter. But she'd spent the last fifteen minutes waving and smiling and chatting with every soul she encountered in the hospital's extended care unit, while he trailed behind her like a queen's obedient servant.

She was doing this to him on purpose, he decided, because she was still irked over the piano business, the reminder of his clairvoyance, and the kiss.

He glared at the back of her head, struggling to balance all the items she'd piled into his arms in the parking lot. He told himself he was acting juvenile. He hadn't really expected her to come back to the inn and fall into his arms, begging him to repeat the experience. Okay, so he'd hoped. He'd get over it.

Like hell he would.

He paused for a second to get a better grip on the heavy, colorfully wrapped and be-ribboned square box. The tower of paperback novels, cloth cosmetic bag, and fancy chocolates piled on top of the box swayed dangerously with the adjustment. A lily sticking out of the huge bouquet of flowers Angie had tucked under his arm goosed his nose. He tried blowing it out of his face but failed.

"Well, *hey* there, darling!" he heard Angie cry with delight.

Fighting off a monumental sneeze and an instant case of jealousy, Gabriel craned his neck to see who had caused her reaction. The only person he saw was an old gentleman in a wheelchair.

Don't stop, don't stop, he silently pleaded. Aw, nuts, she was going to stop.

Angie sashayed up to the fellow. "Are you out here chasing the girls again, you old handsome devil?" she teased, leaning down to throw one arm around his stooped shoulders.

The old gentleman reacted to her charm as though he was being warmed to his bones by pure Virginia sunshine, Gabriel thought. He sat up straight; weariness left the black eyes set in the gnomelike face. He beamed a smile up at her and patted her cheek. "Bless your heart, honey. Oh, I can chase 'em, all right. It's the catching part that gives me grief. I'm not as fast as I used to be."

"Oh poo, you know you're hell on wheels," she said, dropping a kiss on his head. "And I know for a fact that there's one particular lady who has her eye on you." She whispered something in his ear.

He pinked up all the way to his bald head, but his eyes were sparkling like the Fourth of July. He chortled and slapped his knee. "You're just fooling me, girl. That mean old woman won't give me the time of day."

Angie wrinkled her nose and shook her head. "She's just playing hard to get."

Unable to hold it back any longer, Gabriel sneezed three times in rapid succession. His torso shook, disturbing the precarious balance of the items in his arms. The book on top of the pile slipped and fell to the floor.

"Who's your boyfriend, honey?" the elderly man asked, jerking a thumb in Gabriel's direction. "Is he sickly or something?"

Angie looked disconcerted for a moment, then waved a dismissive hand. "Oh, that's just Gabriel. He's visiting from Durham down in North Carolina."

Just. Gabriel sighed inwardly. That was how she'd introduced him to everyone at the hospital.

"Gabriel, this is Mr. Hell-on-Wheels Heyer." She stooped to pick up the book he'd dropped. Smiling wickedly as she rose, she asked, "Are you sickly, Gabe?"

"Uh, no. Pleased to meet you, sir."

"Durham, uh?" Mr. Heyer eyed him curiously. "I was down there once for a Duke game. You a Blue Devil fan?"

"Yes, sir."

"Here you go, doll face," Angie said, handing the book to Mr. Heyer. "This is for you."

He held it up and squinted at the man and woman embracing on the cover. "Is this one of them romance novels?"

"You bet. Read it." She winked at him. "It'll put some zip in your doo-dah. Catch you later."

Mr. Heyer practically popped a wheelie turning the chair around to watch her sashay off. "Not if I catch you first, honey!" he yelled gleefully, no doubt enjoying the way her short pleated skirt flared with each movement of her swaying hips.

Angie just raised one hand and waggled her fingers. She laughed that marvelous silver bell laugh of hers and kept walking on her stiletto heels.

"Ain't she *something*," Mr. Heyer murmured happily.

Gabriel put aside his irritation and looked at Angie with new eyes. The old gentleman was right: She really was something. He had been wrong about her dawdling on purpose. She wasn't trying to irritate him. Angie was just being herself.

For the first time since they'd left the parking lot, he didn't mind being her pack mule. In fact, he was beginning to feel rather proud of the way Angie put smiles on the faces of everyone she met. She'd complimented the women, flirted with the men, and left each and every one of them feeling just a little bit better than they had before.

Pure Virginia sunshine, he thought again. That was Angie. She shone generously and equally on everyone, wrapping them in her warmth. Now how could he resent the sun?

He could do a lot worse, Gabriel decided as he hurried to catch up with her, than to fall for a woman like that.

SIX

Gabriel immediately recognized the hospital room Angie finally led him into. It was the one he'd dreamed about. Two women, sixtyish in age, were there. Ivy Rule was the one laid up in the bed. The other lady, wearing a funny feathered hat and a pinched look of disapproval, was introduced to him as her sister, Clover Norville.

Gabriel immediately liked Miss Ivy, as she insisted he call her. She resembled his ideal image of a grandma, from her snow-white hair to her dimpled smile. If she had shown up at his house, he would have invited her in—no questions asked—to bake cookies in his kitchen. But from the firm way she managed to send her sister home and Angie out into the corridor, he knew she had a bit of steel magnolia in her.

"I hope Clover didn't offend you." Ivy's dimples made a brief but dazzling appearance. "My sister isn't a mean person. She's just been in a bad mood all her life."

Gabriel laughed. "I've been called worse than a 'loose screw.' No offense taken." He sat down in the chair beside her bed. "Are you still interested in monitoring the psychic disturbances going on at the inn?"

"I want you to do more than 'monitor' them." She stretched one hand toward him, and he held it between both of his. "I want you to rescue the Shadow Lady."

"Miss Ivy, I don't know if I can even prove your Shadow Lady exists, much less rescue an earthbound entity. I honestly don't known if *anyone* can." He let go of her hand and rose from the chair.

She held on to his hand.

"Please."

His gaze met hers. Her eyes were the same arresting blue as Angie's and Miles's. It wasn't fair what those eyes could do to him.

Walk through fire for you, my dear? Why, of course!

"That poor tortured spirit wants to be released from this world. You *must* help, Dr. Richards."

Gabriel swallowed a sigh and sealed his fate. "I can't promise results. But I will try."

"Well then, that's all right." She squeezed his hand. "How are you getting on with my niece?"

He thought of the fiery woman he'd held in his arms and kissed only a few hours ago. "Just fine."

"Once you get past her looks, which takes a while for some people, you find she's also got brains. And heart. Lots of heart. I do hope you won't sell her short."

Gabriel met her steady gaze. "I don't suppose," he

said slowly, "that you'd care to give me a hint on how to go about courting your niece?"

She let loose with her irresistible dimples. "State your intentions and be persistent."

"Richards is clean as a whistle," Jake Madison said. He stood with one hand resting lightly upon his wife's shoulder.

Nila Madison, eight months pregnant and still wearing the glow of being deeply in love, smiled up at her husband. "Don't keep Angie in suspense. She's wearing a hole in the carpet."

Angie stopped pacing the waiting room and sat down. "What exactly does 'clean as a whistle' mean? He doesn't have a criminal record? Or he just hasn't been caught doing anything illegal?"

"No criminal record. I can give you a few personal details and observations about him from reliable sources."

She sighed and pushed her hair back from her face. "Gabriel knows I asked someone to check him out. He said it was okay with him. But now I'm not so sure I have any right to know more about him than you've told me already."

"Doesn't sound like he's trying to hide anything," Nila said, absently rubbing her baby-swollen stomach.

"Nor does he act like it," Angie admitted. "I just wish . . ."

What? she asked herself. That she'd met Gabriel under different circumstances? That he was a rocket scientist or a ditchdigger instead of parapsychologist?

"I don't know what I wish." She shied away the confusion swirling inside her.

"I was told that Richards is well respected for his work in the field of ESP," Jake continued. "There are a lot of oddball cranks out there who call themselves psychic investigators or parapsychologists, but he isn't one of them."

She digested that for a moment. "Jake, do you believe in ESP and ghosts?"

"There is more to the cosmos than meets the eye," he answered smoothly. "I think there are senses we have not dreamed of. Richards must be a brave man for daring to champion an intellectually unpopular science."

Angie hadn't thought of him that way. It shed a whole new light upon the man.

An hour later Angie took Gabriel to Short Sugars for lunch. The restaurant was noisy and packed, but they were quickly shown to a table.

After a waitress took their order, Angie fished in her handbag, found a cigarette, and lit it. Sitting back, she studied Gabriel. She absorbed the clean contours of his face and the solemnness of the wide span of his mouth. His mysterious eyes didn't begin to reveal his inner complexity.

Jake's words echoed in her mind. *A brave man.*

She had walked into the hospital with one conception of Gabriel, and she had walked out with another. All she was left with now were her own prejudices—and a strong liking for the man who was the source of them.

She remembered how she'd felt when he'd kissed her that morning. Oh, all right. As long as she was being honest with herself, she might as well admit it was more than a strong liking; it was a confounded sexual attraction that seemed to grow stronger by the minute.

Turning her thoughts away from that, she flicked ashes into a cheap metal ashtray. "I'll say this for you, Gabriel Richards, you don't gloat. You're a good winner."

"You have my respect for not pouting." His eyes reflected the sudden smile that flirted across his mouth.

She shrugged with as much nonchalance as she could muster in the face of that heart-stopping smile. "A done deal is a done deal. Pouting would be childish and silly." She really hadn't had any choice but to cooperate with her aunt and Gabriel. "I suppose it won't kill me to spend a few more weeks living at the inn, watching you play ghostbuster."

"I'm glad you agreed to stay on. Thank you." His gaze briefly touched her lips and stole her breath, then lifted to probe her eyes, as though searching for whatever emotions they might communicate.

"Don't thank me." She stubbed out the cigarette and

dropped it into the ashtray. "I still think the whole thing is a truckload of bull dooty."

"I know your opinion hasn't changed." He stretched his hand across the small table to cover hers.

She glanced down at their hands. His grip was surprisingly strong, the tips of his fingers surprisingly gentle as they stroked her wrist. Erratic heartbeats filled her throat.

"And it won't change," she said firmly. "I'm only doing this because Ivy begged me to. That's all."

"I still appreciate the fact that you're willing to support your aunt's decision."

He released her hand, his fingertips trailing a slow caress over the back of it and between her fingers. Angie's heartbeats quickened as her body acknowledged the tug on her senses. Rational thoughts were engulfed by heightened sensations. It was as though she and Gabriel were completely alone.

Through the wasteland of her reason, she saw his curious gaze fix upon her in that odd, searching way of his. In his study of her she read interest, a touch of longing, and something that might, on the deepest plane, have been regret. Even as she wondered what the regret might be for, she realized with a jolt that he was finding her as desirable and emotionally puzzling as she found him.

The arrival of the waitress with their meals enabled her to retreat from that knowledge.

As she busied herself with the task of eating, the

sensible side of her personality told the vulnerable side to shape up. It was okay to go along for the ride and spend a few weeks hanging around while he chased an imaginary ghost. It wasn't okay to let her hormones complicate the situation.

She simply wouldn't act on her desire for him. Granted, she was a flirt; she loved to flirt. But her self-respect would never allow her to involve herself in a situation that could lead to meaningless, casual sex—no matter how great the temptation, she thought as she shot a veiled glance at Gabriel.

The relationship between them could be friendly—fun, even—but not complex enough to cause problems. After all, he was just passing through her life.

And he was a ghostbuster. Her prejudice against what he did for a living rose up and made the food she'd just put in her mouth tasteless.

Gabriel savored a bite of his spareribs. The barbecue sauce was excellent, spicy but not too hot. He started to remark upon it to Angie, but he looked up and saw that she seemed distracted and uneasy. She was fiddling with the coleslaw on her plate, pushing it around with her fork.

He wiped his mouth on a napkin. "You're not eating. Are you upset?"

"No. I'm just not as hungry as I thought I was. When I'm upset, you'll definitely know it." She flashed a smile that caused the fragment of a song to pop into his mind, something about sunshine and pure desire.

Since he had something to discuss with her that he knew was going to upset her, he decided he'd best be prepared. "How will I know when you're upset?"

"After I get through screaming, I'll reach for a cigarette." She laughed at the face he made.

"Try reaching for something else instead."

"Like what?" she asked dryly.

"My hand."

Gabriel was amused by his own romantic whimsy, an element he didn't know he possessed. But he was serious, dead serious, about wanting to be the comfort she needed whenever she felt upset.

"Want to give it a try?" he asked, holding out his hand, palm up.

She shook her head, evading his gaze. "I told you, I'm not upset."

"Then why are you so pensive?"

"I'm contemplating my prejudices, if you must know, Mr. Nosy."

"What about them?"

She pushed her plate to one side, then took her tea glass in both hands and stared down into it. "I don't like to think of myself as having any."

"No one does." He wondered what mysterious thoughts she was hiding behind her lashes.

He could often discern all the subtle shades of emotion a person was feeling. But, for some reason, hers remained secret from him at the moment. Could it be because his own feelings were blocking his ability to tune in to hers?

She still would not look at him. "I've always pro-claimed I don't have any prejudices, but I've just realized that I do."

Where are you leading with this, Angie?

"I suppose," he answered carefully, "that everyone has at least one, whether it concerns food, race, creed, or any of a million other ridiculous things."

She glanced up. Her expression was sincere, but her cheek carried a flush of embarrassment.

"Ridiculous things," she repeated. "I nominate the ban against the wearing of white shoes after Labor Day for the Ridiculous Prejudice Hall of Fame."

He grinned. "Personally, I can't tolerate cars painted puke green. I don't much care about what kind of auto-mobile I drive, but there's something about cars that color that makes me want to write nasty letters to who-ever made them."

That drew a soft laugh from her.

"What other prejudices are you contemplating?" he asked.

"Well, I can't tolerate liars, cheats, hypocrites, pre-tentious people, or sauerkraut." She shrugged, and the golden waterfall of her hair shifted, then resettled around her shoulders. "I always considered the first four justified and the last a matter of taste. But maybe they're really prejudices in disguise. What I didn't know until you showed up at the inn was that . . ." Her voice trailed off.

She looked embarrassed again. And a little nervous,

he thought as he glanced at her fingers. They kept fanning out from the glass between her hands, then curling around it.

He took an educated guess on the prejudice she was having trouble admitting to. "If you're trying to tell me that you're intolerant of anything that smacks of the supernatural, I'm already aware of it."

"Not terribly open-minded of me, I know. But that's the way I feel."

"Are you afraid of ghosts?"

"No, I'm not afraid." Impatience flashed in her eyes. "I put ghosts in the same category as flying saucers. They make for highly entertaining stories told around a camp fire, provided one does not take those stories too seriously."

"Therefore, your intolerance extends to people who take the subject of ghosts too seriously." He smiled wryly. "Like *me*."

She blushed. "Hearing you say that makes me feel a bit petty. But yes, I'm afraid so."

"Perhaps closer acquaintance with me and with the way I work will help you form a more favorable opinion," he suggested hopefully.

"Maybe." She didn't sound convinced.

Gabriel buttered a roll. Thinking of Miss Ivy's advice, he decided this was as good a time as any to state his intentions. "I hope so, because I'd like a chance to become something more than a stranger to you."

His breath caught and hurt. There it was, out in the open. What would she do with it?

Angie didn't pretend that she didn't understand what he was asking of her. His expression said even more than his straightforward words. Upon that handsome face, she saw naked longing.

Her thoughts became storm-tossed, consumed in a wistful longing that came from senses long dormant. She fought and won an inner battle of emotions.

"Gabriel, you're a nice guy," she began tentatively. "But—"

"You said you liked nice guys," he interrupted, wagging the roll in his hand at her.

She laughed. "Yes, I did say that. And I do like you, Mr. Nice Guy." *Too much for comfort.* "I'm flattered. Really. But please understand that what you want can never be. My attitude toward what you do for a living may not be fair or justifiable, but it's there and it's real. It would stand in the way of anything more than friendship."

He studied her, his feelings open and briefly readable. What she saw unstrung her to her heart. It suddenly occurred to her that this brilliant, complex man was as lonely as she. They could have been mirrors reflecting the same emotion at each other.

"Never say never to a scientist," he said at last. "We thrive on the challenge of proving impossible theories."

"Feelings and impossible theories are two different things."

"You worry too much, pretty lady." The sensual heat in his gaze was even more difficult to resist than the glint of humor she liked so much.

She cleared her throat and changed the subject. "So, Gabe, how do you go about hunting a ghost?"

"I'd rather talk about that kiss—"

"No." Her voice shook. "I'd rather not."

He sighed and gave in graciously. "One of the first things we need to do is to confirm the physical presence of the entity at the inn. Is it in the mind of the person? Or is it a real physical presence?"

"How do we go about confirming something that isn't?"

"Scientifically, of course." He seemed amused. "We record any change in the physical environment: sound, sight, heat, field magnetic changes. Since we don't know what makes ghosts appear, or if they only appear when human beings are present, I'll set up recording equipment and infrared cameras and leave them on continuously."

"Okay, that seems simple enough. Then what? Do we just sit around and wait?"

Gabriel grinned. "Are you sure you don't want to talk about that kiss?" he asked, flashing on the kiss they'd shared, then conjuring up some steamy images of what they could do instead of sitting around and waiting.

"Absolutely not." A blush rose in her cheeks, and he sensed her thoughts were traveling along the same lines as his. That pleased him enormously. She might not want to talk about that kiss, but she was definitely thinking about it.

"Okay." He cooled his inner visions with a huge gulp of iced tea. "You could help me out by doing some research for me. I'd say the Shadow Lady falls into the category of continuous apparition—one that appears repeatedly in the same place. One theory suggests that type of apparition returns to the place where his or her violent death occurred."

She wrinkled her nose. "Sounds gruesome. What am I supposed to research?"

"The history of the house and its occupants. Find out if anyone has ever died violently there."

"That covers a lot of years, Gabe." She gave him a dubious look. "The house was built in 1892 by a man named Charles Kingston."

"Then Kingston is your starting point. Check the library and historical archives. See how far back the local newspaper has stored its back issues on microfiche. Any information you could come up with could help us get a handle on what happened to whom, and when."

"All right. I have some free time this afternoon. I'll go to the library and see if there's anything pertinent in the local history files."

"Take Miles with you." He grinned. "He's a great researcher."

"He's done quite enough research, thank you very much. Are you about ready to go?"

"Angie, about Miles . . ."

Gabriel closed his mouth. Now that he'd come to the sticking point, he found he'd rather walk naked down Main Street than upset her.

"What about Miles?"

His professionalism struggled with his personal interests for a moment. "Would you like dessert?"

"No thanks. But go ahead and order some, if you want."

"I really don't want any either." He pushed his plate to the side and sat back.

"Why are you frowning?" she asked. "If you have something to tell me about my son, then get on with it."

He shook his head and folded his arms. "I'm about to tread on sensitive toes, that's why I'm frowning. I hate like hell to do it."

She frowned. "I hate it when people preamble bad news with statements like that. You're making me nervous."

"As a scientist, I am required to approach my subject matter objectively, with a certain skepticism, if you will." He didn't want to go on, but he had no choice. "You know I like Miles very much."

Her frown deepened. Already, he could see she didn't like what he might be leading up to.

Gabriel held back a sigh. "Miss Ivy and Miles have both reported seeing the movement of physical objects that they've attributed to the entity. But it has been my experience, as well as the experience of other reputable parapsychologists, that such incidents are produced by the *living* rather than the dead. Usually it can be associated with a particular person."

An odd expression came across her face, part fear and part comprehension. "Gabe, you've got to do something about this tendency to be verbose. It's annoying. What's your point? And what does it have to do with my son?"

He was going to hurt her and he was deeply sorry. "The person at the center of these phenomena is frequently young—often adolescent—with unstable emotions."

Her mouth tightened. She looked like she felt a scream and a nicotine fit coming on.

He lowered his gaze. "There is almost always a built-up and powerful, but repressed, anger and hostility. An inability to express rage becomes crippling, and the child is rarely aware of that repression." He looked at her and gentled his voice. "Miles could be causing the psychic disturbances without being aware he is doing it."

Angie was shocked to the core at what he was suggesting about her baby. She felt sharp spots of heat in her cheeks. The heat turned to ice, but she didn't flinch as she stared at him.

His features were somber in the neon light that glared down from the ceiling fixtures. Her palms itched to smack that Boy Scout face.

Instead, she reached for her cigarettes and lighter. She lit one and took a drag. When she could speak calmly, she said, "Has anyone ever told you what a pain in the neck you can be?"

Gabriel didn't answer. He just watched the wisp of smoke curling from her cigarette, and he felt just as upset as she. Sometimes it wasn't easy to maintain his scientists's objectivity. This was one of those times. To the depths of his soul he wished he hadn't had to tread on the most vulnerable part of her—her son.

They fell silent. Behind them a baby began to cry. Its screams rose in a crescendo that matched the scream welling up inside Angie. Finally, mother and baby went outside, which Angie decided would be a wise thing for her to do as well.

Getting up, she doused her cigarette and dug into her purse for her wallet. She threw some money down on the table, and then without a backward glance, left the restaurant.

SEVEN

Gabriel sat outside on the covered terrace, worrying about Angie as he waited for her to return. It was almost dark. It had been over four hours since she'd driven him back to the inn and left him there without saying a word.

Never had he felt so disgusted with himself as he did for hurting her at lunch. What made it even more disgusting was the knowledge that if he had it to do over again, he would have handled the situation the same way. He sighed and lifted one hand to massage the ache trip-hammering against his temple.

Worrying about someone besides himself was a different and rather excruciating experience. In fact, falling in love was worse than he'd imagined. A thousand times . . .

Falling in love? Was that what he was doing?

He sat very still for a long moment, listening to the

wind shudder around the house as though desperately trying to get in. His nerves were raw from an assault of emotion. Just like the wind, he felt like he was struggling to get in—in to Angie's life.

The sight of her red convertible coming up the long driveway flooded him with relief. He tucked his previous thoughts away, to be taken out later for further examination.

The passenger door flew open the moment the car came to a stop. Miles bounced out, holding his cat, and rushed toward Gabriel like a small tornado. "Hi! Mama says you're staying. I'm so glad."

"So am I." He smiled down at the boy, then glanced up to meet Angie's gaze. He sensed she was no longer angry with him, but he couldn't read her emotions.

"Have you set up the surveillance equipment?" the boy asked eagerly.

"Yes, I have. You may go look at it, if you want."

"Thank you!" Miles gave him one of his radiant smiles. "I won't touch anything. Promise." He and the cat disappeared through the front door.

Burdened with a bag of groceries and a manila folder, Angie approached more sedately than her son. A tightness settled in Gabriel's chest as he noted her subdued expression.

"Let me take that for you," he said, going down the steps to meet her. She handed over the grocery sack.

Neither of them moved for a second as they stared at each other uncomfortably.

"Angie—"

"Gabe—" she began at the same time.

"I'm sorry." His voice was calm. His muscles were tight. "I was worried about you."

"I'm fine."

Gabriel was hit with an overwhelming urge to drop the paper bag and take her in his arms. He settled for raising one hand to her hair. It was silky and thick, and his fingers begged to curl it around his hand.

She tipped her face up to his, her blue eyes mesmerizing him. "I'm sorry for getting so upset. It's just that I'm very sensitive where Miles is concerned." For a second she looked pale, drained, as she had at the restaurant. Smothering an oath, Gabriel moved closer to her. Before he could speak, she continued in a calm, direct voice, "I don't believe Miles is the cause of the disturbances supposedly going on here, any more than I believe in ghosts. But just to prove you wrong, starting tomorrow morning he's going to stay with Nila and Jake for a few days."

"Nothing would please me more than for you to prove me wrong."

"Good. That's settled." She smiled at him for the first time since they'd left the restaurant.

Need swept through him. He cupped the back of her head with his hand. "There's something else we have to settle too. Every time I look into your eyes, I feel like I've been struck by lightning."

Angie felt her heart skip a beat.

"I think I could resist you," he went on, "if there were a dull-witted brain behind your beautiful face. Or if you had a shallow personality instead of being vibrant and caring."

Something warm poured through her like a lazy river.

"I don't know much about courting a woman." His voice was tender, almost a murmur. "I envision quiet dinners, candlelight, and flowers. Does that sound right?"

"It sounds nice," she managed after a moment. A tiny smile tipped the corners of her mouth. "I do believe you have a streak of romance in . . ."

Her voice trailed off as she found herself swaying closer to him. So close. It was his breath, his heat she felt on her skin rather than the sultry early-evening air. Every sensitive place on her body seemed to come alive, begging for his touch.

"Then I have your permission to court you?" The sweet, old-fashioned simplicity of his words cloaked her heart with tenderness.

Angie very badly wanted to throw common sense to the wind, even though she knew it wasn't smart to operate on emotion alone. Still, she couldn't force the word "no" past her lips. "You're only going to be here for a short time."

A grin furrowed little laugh wrinkles at the corners of his mouth, but his eyes were serious. "Anything can happen in four weeks."

She didn't want to argue. If she were to win out over

her emotions, she needed to be strong. "Well, that's certainly something to think about. Let's go inside. I need to start dinner."

Gabriel didn't press the issue. He'd seen the flash of vulnerability in her eyes and had sensed her longing to throw caution to the wind. As Ivy Rule had advised him, he'd stated his intentions. Next he'd work on his persistence.

Keep it light for now, he told himself. "Should I be prepared to weep for joy at your dinner table tonight?"

"Darling," she drawled in a honeyed magnolia voice that no woman north of the Mason-Dixon line could ever hope to reproduce, "warm up your tear ducts."

He laughed and moved aside so she could precede him up the steps.

By the time he retired to his room for the evening, Gabriel realized he shouldn't have laughed. He'd dined on sliced chicken breasts, seasoned and sautéed to perfection, mushrooms stuffed with artichoke hearts, and crepes with raspberry sauce.

Yes indeed. A man could do a lot worse than to fall in love with a woman who cooked like Julia Child and who generated more sexual heat than Marilyn Monroe.

The dream began as soon as Gabriel fell asleep. He saw himself in a room other than his own. He didn't know why he was there, he only knew that *someone* wanted him to be there.

His gaze traveled over the large, high-ceilinged boudoir, taking in an enormous four-poster and an armoire made of what he thought was rosewood. a rococo gilt mirror hung above an old-fashioned vanity table. Cosmetic brushes with silver handles lay on the vanity, along with an ornate silver hand mirror, cut-glass perfume bottles, and a black velvet hair ribbon. A couple of chairs and a small settee in shades of rose, cream, and soft blue were grouped around a brick fireplace. Two silver vases filled with pastel silk roses rested upon the white marble mantel, one at each end, along with two heavy silver candlesticks.

What impressed Gabriel most about the room was the light scent of roses. He once more had the feeling that someone or something wanted him to be there, that he'd been drawn to this room for a purpose.

Hearing the tinkling sound of glass upon glass, he looked up. A pewter-and-glass chandelier hung above the bed. Prisms dangling from the six etched glass globes trembled and swayed as though they were leaves touched by the wind.

A sense of dread filling him, he lowered his gaze to the bed. A woman lay sleeping there. Warmth replaced the apprehension he had felt as he recognized Angie.

He was momentarily spellbound by glimpses of smooth, pale skin and the gentle rise and fall of her breasts beneath white silk as she breathed the shallow breath of slumber. Then her long blonde hair captured his attention. It spilled across the lace-edged pillow like fine silk, and he was shocked by an intense desire to experience the purely sensual pleasure of rubbing a strand between his fingers.

With her lovely, delicate features, she reminded him of Sleeping Beauty. One small hand rested beside her cheek, her fingers curled inward, and her lips were slightly parted, as though waiting for a kiss to awaken her. The whimsical thought made him smile. He was no Prince Charming, but he wanted to be the one who rescued her with a kiss from the witch's evil spell.

Overhead the glass prisms began to shake more violently, drawing his gaze upward again. Breath hitched in his chest as he realized the chandelier was hanging directly over Angie.

The sense of dread returned. He had to wake her. Warn her that she was in danger.

He tried to move but could not.

He shouted her name over and over. She did not hear.

He willed her to wake up. She slept on.

Above her the chandelier swung wildly to and fro.

Heart pounding, he understood he could do nothing, could only stand by helplessly, waiting and watching.

Again and again his gaze returned to the chandelier. It continued to tremble and sway. He imagined it rocking so violently that it tore away from the ceiling.

If it should fall . . .

Gabriel awoke abruptly to a wave of nausea. Gasping

for breath, he sat up and rolled off the bed. He fumbled for the lamp on the bedside table.

The cat was the first thing he saw when the light came on. Sugar Booger flipped onto his back and stared up at Gabriel, then began to purr in a deep baritone as though asking what was happening.

"The dream was a warning." Gabriel ran a shaky hand across his face.

Something was going to happen to Angie. He knew it as clearly as he knew his own name.

The compelling need to stop the dream event from happening in reality obliterated everything, from rational thoughts to the sound of rain thrashing against the windows and wind rustling through the eaves of the house.

He grabbed the jeans he'd earlier draped over the back of a brocade chaise longue. Hobbling across the floor, he yanked them on. Not bothering with shoes or shirt, he zipped his pants with one hand while turning the doorknob with the other.

His heart raced faster than his bare feet on the oriental carpet along the hallway.

His only thought was of Angie. He had to reach her in time.

Angie was aware of the strength and warmth of his flesh as she walked hand in hand with him along the fieldstone path. She glanced around in amazement at the area on the north border of Ivy's property.

It should have been a jungle of tangled vines, weeds, and shrubs, but it wasn't. She knew she must be seeing it for the well-tended garden it once had been. Why, even the white-latticed gazebo stood as strong as the day it had been built.

Being with *him* made her feel so good, she didn't stop to question the how or why of these things. Just as she had no desire to wonder where the scent of roses was coming from, though she didn't think roses had ever been grown there.

Perhaps the fragrance permeating the air was simply a part of being in love. Angie breathed in the pleasant aroma and felt glad to be alive. Glad just to be with him.

The feeling of being in love again gave her such joy, she wanted to laugh out loud. She wanted to dance, not walk solemnly, toward their destination.

Destination?

Some rational part of her subconscious knew it was only a dream, but she didn't care. She simply wanted it to go on and on.

Being in love again was her most secret desire. Her deepest need. Her greatest source of fear.

Once she'd known the most all-encompassing love, and death had snatched it away from her while it was still fresh and new. She feared never knowing that kind of soul-deep love in her life again. Just as she feared growing old alone.

A sound intruded upon the dream.

Angie fought wakefulness. She didn't want to leave the warm cocoon of slumber. She didn't want to trade the beautiful dream for lonely, waking reality.

The noise grew louder.

Her dream lover and the garden began to shimmer and fade.

Angie came awake with a start.

For a moment, she lay still. A keen sense of loss formed a painful knot inside her as she listened to the falling rain, the rumble of thunder, and . . .

A fist pounding on her door?

Sleepy eyes at half-mast, she raised up on her elbows. The Waterford crystal clock on the nightstand showed three o'clock.

The pounding persisted.

Her first thought was of Miles. Was her baby ill? Frightened by a nightmare?

She threw back the bed linens. Her feet had barely touched the floor, when the sleep-fog lifted from her mind.

It couldn't be Miles at the door. His small hand was not capable of making such a racket. Besides, her son wouldn't knock. He would just come in and wake her.

Hesitantly, she crossed the room and placed one hand on the door. "Who is it?" she called out, switching on the overhead light. Her eyes blinked in the sudden glare.

The knocking ceased. "It's me, Gabriel. I need to speak with you, Angie. It's urgent."

Her brow furrowed at the frantic note she heard in his voice, then alarm spread through her. There was only one reason a guest would be pounding on her door at this hour.

The house was on fire!

Sheer black fright swept through her, along with images of smoke and flames. "Where is it?" she screeched, throwing the door wide open.

"Thank God, you're safe."

"Where's the fire?" Hopping up and down, she craned her neck to see over Gabriel's shoulder into the hallway beyond. She sniffed the air and wondered why the smoke detectors were ominously silent.

"What fire?" he asked, sounding distant and confused.

"Dammit, Gabe, wake up and get with the program!" She grabbed his arm and shook it. "The fire you came to tell me about. Don't just stand there. Call the fire department."

"Angie, I—"

Her gaze narrowed on his face. His eyes were open wide, but they seemed unfocused. He also appeared rooted to the floor. "Oh, for crying out loud, Gabe. Snap out of it, or we're all going to be fried to a crisp!"

She started to brush by him. He blocked her path.

"Angie, wait—"

"Move it," she growled. "We've got to get out of here!" Shoving at him with her forearm, she caught him off guard enough to drive him back a step.

He lunged for her as she dove past him. His arms encircled her waist and he pulled her against him.

"Let go! I've got to wake Miles."

"There's no fire," he yelled, catching her flailing arms in his hands. "Listen to me, Angie. There's *no* fire."

She stopped struggling. "No fire?" she asked blankly, twisting in his arms to look up at him.

He shook his head and released her. "I'm sorry. It didn't occur to me that you would think—"

"Where are your brains, genius?" she hissed, bopping him on the head with the heel of her palm. "What else was I supposed to think?"

"You didn't have to hit me." He rubbed his forehead, his expression as sulky as that of a little boy who thought himself unjustly accused and punished. "I said I was sorry."

"Well, 'Sorry' doesn't cut it, mister."

Gabriel saw that there was definitely a fire now. It was in her eyes. He smiled. She was safe. That was more important than her being mad at him.

"Of all the confounded, irritating men I've ever met, you're the most . . . most confounding and . . . and irritating," she sputtered. "Do you know what time it is? It's three o'clock in the morning. What in the world possessed you to come beat on my door and scare me half to death?"

Pausing only to push her tangled hair back from her face, she rushed on before he could get a word in. "I swear, I'm beginning to think Aunt Clover is right. *Men* have got to be the most useless, annoying creatures on this green earth. The Good Lord must have been out of his mind when he created . . ." And on she went.

Gabriel made no attempt to save himself from a verbal reaming by interrupting. He simply stopped listening to her. He knew she was just relieved and didn't mean a word of what she was saying. At least, he hoped she wasn't serious about kicking his butt out into the street and tossing his clothes out after him.

"Are you listening to me?"

"Uh-huh." He glanced around her bedroom. It was the same one he'd dreamed about. Everything was exactly the same, from the color scheme to the feminine items spread out over the vanity table to the gilt mirror hanging above it.

"Gabe?"

He sniffed the air as he moved farther into the chamber. The scent of roses was absent.

Swallowing heavily, he looked at the enormous four-poster and the chandelier directly above it. The pewter-and-glass light fixture was completely still.

"You are *not* listening!"

He gave her a distracted glance over his shoulder. She stood in the open doorway, hands on her hips, her eyes shooting sparks of anger.

For the first time, he noticed the shorty pajamas she was wearing. White silky fabric skimmed over her feminine curves, outlined the aroused peaks of her breasts, and showed off long, slim legs. And it bothered him in the nicest possible way. She was without doubt the most uncommon and utterly beautiful woman he had ever laid eyes on. He would have liked nothing more in that moment than to lay her beneath him and kiss every inch of her lovely fair skin.

"Are you all right? Is something wrong?" She stared at him with concern.

Gabriel got hold of himself. "I'm fine," he said, answering her question and stalling for time.

How was he going to explain his bizarre behavior? Long ago, he'd learned not to blurt out the things he saw or felt psychically. Seeing what others couldn't and knowing what wasn't his to know led to difficulties. He couldn't think of a time when he'd been in a more difficult position than now.

His troubled gaze returned to the chandelier.

No trembling. No tinkling of glass prisms.

And he began to doubt.

Perhaps he'd misinterpreted the dream, read too much into it. Maybe he'd wanted to be with Angie so badly, his subconscious had given him an excuse to seek her out. Hell, maybe he'd just had a nightmare.

Behind him, Angie fought the temptation to just stand there and contemplate the sight of his broad shoulders, his strong, straight back, and the dark hair curling behind his ears. But she conquered it and looked everywhere but at him. Dignity forbade that she risk being discovered peeping at him in admiration like a lovesick girl.

She went over and touched his shoulder. "Gabe? Are you sure you're all right?"

He half-turned and met her gaze. His mysterious gray eyes were filled with what she interpreted as nervous dread. Then an expression of grim, stoic resignation stole over his face. "I dreamed something was going to happen to you. I thought you were in danger."

"You dreamed I was in danger?"

"I know it sounds fantastic, crazy."

She let her hand drop. The very idea of Gabriel rushing to her side in an attempt to rescue her sent a warm glow flowing through her. No one, not even her beloved husband Jon, had ever considered her as someone in need of protection or rescue in any circumstances—real or imagined. She had always been the defender, the one who wouldn't hesitate to fight dragons or tilt at windmills for the people she loved.

Abruptly, she realized Gabriel was looking at her as though he were waiting in dread for the ax to fall. "It doesn't sound crazy," she said softly. "In fact, I'm touched. No one has ever gotten up in the middle of the night to check on me because they dreamed I was in danger."

He stared at her. Angie saw he was plainly astonished, and realized, ruefully, that he wasn't the only one. But she wasn't going to retract her words.

"You believe me?"

"Of course." She smiled warmly at him. "Gabe, I do believe you have a chivalrous streak. I forgive you for scaring me."

"You're full of surprises. I never know what to expect from you." He caught her hand in his and pressed it to his lips.

"Gabe . . ."

Whatever she'd meant to say was lost as her gaze made an involuntary traverse of his body, where lean muscles and supple skin gave exquisite form to jeans he'd obviously donned in haste. She began to feel shaky inside, and marveled that he had the power to enthrall her so.

"What?"

"What?" she repeated, glancing up to meet his gaze.

"You said my name."

"Oh, yes." She wanted to force the tension from her body, but looking at him was like standing before a banquet table after years of starvation. "I forgot what I was going to say."

Gabriel shivered as urgent threads of desire wrapped tightly around him. He sensed she was more aware of him now as a man than she had ever been before. And he wanted that, needed it.

"Are you cold?" she asked.

He sucked in his breath when she slipped her hand up over his chest and neck to briefly lay the tips of her fingers upon his cheek.

"No." He was burning with a desire that would give him no serenity if he couldn't have her.

She was watching him curiously, though she was smiling. That smile made him acutely conscious of her mouth, of its color and shape, of how her lips felt soft and satiny, moist and wistful.

"I wish you wouldn't look at me that way," she said. She lowered her gaze, but not before he'd seen a flash of panic, mingled with embarrassment.

"What way?" Like a geeky kid lusting after the freshman class beauty? Like a fool falling in love?

"You don't look, you stare so intensely." She looked up at him from beneath her fringe of dark lashes. "It's like you can see everything that I am, inside and outside."

"It's hard not to stare at you." Was that really his voice? he wondered. It sounded too warm, thick, strange. "You're lovely. Inside and out. I think I could stare at you for days, years." *Forever.*

Her questioning gaze held fast to his.

"That was a compliment." He tried to keep out of his voice the desire winding ever tighter around him. "You're supposed to accept it and say thank you."

"Thank you."

"You're welcome." He lifted one finger to the undercurve of her chin, testing with a gentle stroke, watching her eyes. She had no resistance. He could see it in her eyes, feel it in the various shades of emotions emanating from her.

She shied away from his gaze.

"There's no need to be nervous, pretty lady."

She glanced back at him, whispering, "It frustrates me not to know your thoughts the way you seem to know mine."

He was absorbed in her face, following the contours and planes with his finger. He spoke as softly as she had. "It was a fluke, that one time I knew what you were thinking. I'm good at reading emotions, not minds."

"That's just as . . . dangerous." The last word was more than a breath, less than a whisper.

"I'm never careless with others' emotions. Never."

"Romantic. Chivalrous. And now honorable." Her smile was restless, full of ardent whimsy.

Gabriel's thoughts began to evaporate under the pressure of wanting to take her in his arms, bring her closer. . . . He leaned forward, touching his mouth lightly to hers.

First she moved not at all. Then her breath came quickly on his mouth in a motionless kiss. Saying his name as though it were a prayer, she swayed closer to him.

He lifted his hands to her shoulders, drawing her to him slowly. Kneading her flesh beneath the white silk, he brought them together so that his body caressed her breasts and stomach. The thin fabric veiling her heightened his sensations, and all he knew was the heat of her lips and the pain of wanting her.

Too strong, too intense, Angie thought, clinging now to an open-mouth kiss. She was flying, passing through the universe she knew into one full of mystery and urgent heat and passion. He slipped one hand to her hip, trailed it higher, finding entrance under the layer of cloth. His palm was warm and sweet on her skin.

He lifted his mouth a fraction away from hers. She heard his breath whisper out in a pleasured sigh.

"This doesn't make sense." She slid her hands over his chest and shakily began massaging the supple flesh with her fingers. His skin seemed to grow warm, silken.

Pulling back to meet her gaze, he said, "If only you knew what was inside me now, you'd know it's the only thing that does make sense."

She looked up at him through the mist created by the deep passion stirring within her. Her pulse raced furiously with the questions forming in her mind. "I don't understand."

"Neither do I." He nuzzled her lower lip, making it tremble. His body shifted slightly, sparking pleasure all through her. His chest and hips pressed against hers with sweet strength, then his mouth was questing against hers, his lips urging hers into moist compliance. His tongue touched the inside of her mouth.

Shivers spread up her back. Angie felt weaker and warmer by the second. Gabriel was kissing her as though there was nothing else he would rather be doing, as though nothing else existed but that single-minded pleasure.

Her body arched instinctively against his hardening length, encouraged by his hungry kisses and caresses. A part of her couldn't help wanting him, even though she could feel a faint lingering resistance in her mind.

She eased her mouth from his, brushing a last kiss over his cheek before turning her head away.

Sensing her sudden reluctance, Gabriel gave a wavering sigh. "Kissing you is amazing. Sinfully erotic. It's a miracle I can still stand."

Her eyes were wide. The expression in them matched her tiny smile—sort of dreamy or longing, he wasn't sure which. He didn't doubt she wanted him, but he wanted more than that from her. He wanted her to care for him.

She said nothing, just stood there looking at him with her dreamer's eyes. She seemed more fragile to him now, more unsure of herself than he'd thought possible. His heart would have gone out to her in sympathy, if it hadn't been so busy turning upside down and inside out.

He wanted to say the right thing to her, but it was difficult to think coherently. He took a breath, hoping to clear his head. It didn't do any good. He just kept on feeling the hot sparks of desire, a symphony of loving emotion prickling in his blood.

Unable to continue meeting his gaze, Angie lowered her eyes to the smooth expanse of his chest. That turned out to be a big mistake, for she couldn't resist the temptation to visually trace the faint line of dark hair that began in the region of his belly button and disappeared beneath the waistband of his loose-fitting jeans.

Her eyes closed as a potent emotion fluttered in her stomach. Heavenly days! It wasn't fair that she should suddenly find even his belly button sexually arousing. She was definitely on the verge of developing a foolish—but not fatal, she hoped—craving for him.

She tried to combat that craving by reminding herself that he spent his life pursuing things beyond the comprehension of limited human senses. She didn't need that kind of complication in her life. She had enough trouble just trying to make sense of ordinary human existence. That alone was enough to make any romantic involvement between them impossible. Added to that was the fact that intellectually she didn't come close to playing in his league.

Unfortunately, none of those reminders seemed to have any bearing on her emotions.

"Gabe." She stepped back. "A gentleman always knows when it's time to leave a lady's bedroom." She strove to keep her tone light and teasing.

Releasing her, he dropped his arms back to his sides. "Angie, I—" He stopped speaking abruptly.

She watched him stiffen, as though something had suddenly alarmed him. The expression on his face changed, became distant.

Believing what she saw was wounded male pride, she said gently, "I enjoyed what we just shared, Gabe. But it can't go any further tonight. I hope you understand."

He stared at her.

"Do you smell roses?"

EIGHT

The question startled Angie almost as much as the harsh intensity with which Gabriel had spoken. His gaze darted around the room as though he were searching for the source of the scent.

"Roses?" she repeated uncertainly.

"Not real flowers." He lifted his head, taking a deep draft of air. "It's more like the perfume my grandmother wore. Rose water, she called it."

"I don't smell anything." She frowned as something tickled her memory: the dream. "But it's odd that—" She stopped herself from blurting out that the scent of roses had prevailed in her dream.

"What's odd?" he asked, giving her a sharp glance.

"It's nothing really."

He moved swiftly, capturing her shoulders in his hands. "Tell me. It may be important."

She frowned at him, not understanding his agitation.

"I told you, it was nothing. Just a dream I was having when you pounded on my door."

"A dream," he repeated, easing his grip on her shoulders. "Tell me about it. Please." He slid his hands down her arms to her wrists. When he brought her hands up to rest on his chest, she could feel the frantic racing of his heart.

Angie told him about dreaming she was walking in the garden, but edited out the parts about the lover and her feeling of being in love.

"Are there rosebushes in that area now?" he asked with some urgency when she finished.

"No. I remember thinking it was strange, because I don't think those flowers were ever grown there. It's too shady."

Gabriel's heartbeat quickened as the rose scent began to fill the room. There was something significant about Angie's dream. He wished he could think straight long enough to know what the hell it was.

"That part of the property has been neglected forever," she continued, her melodious voice beginning to sound as far away as starlight. "There's nothing there now but overgrown shrubs, vines, and a tumbled-down gazebo."

The subtle fragrance grew stronger. Gabriel stirred restlessly, breathing it into his lungs, his senses.

The entity was here.

Letting go of Angie's wrists, he pivoted. His gaze scanned the room from floor to ceiling, wall to wall.

She—the Shadow Lady—was here with them.

A flash of excitement vanished as quickly as it had come. The dread he'd felt in his dream invaded his mind, his muscles.

"I've been meaning to hire someone to clear out that area for Aunt Ivy." The sound of Angie's voice, the drone of the rain outside, the pounding of his heart all registered in a distant corner of his mind.

Then he heard it.

The tinkle of crystal.

Sweat formed on his brow as he slowly looked up.

"What is that noise?"

"The chandelier," he whispered. The pewter-and-glass fixture swayed gently, as though rocked by an unseen hand. Crystal prisms hanging elegantly from the six etched globes trembled, their soft tinkling sound like wind chimes.

He glanced at Angie. Didn't she feel the impending dread of *something* about to happen? She was studying the light fixture with puzzled fascination, seeming not at all alarmed.

"How odd," she said. "What's making it do that?"

He didn't respond as he looked at the chandelier again. The prisms began to shake more violently, until the whole chandelier swung as though it were being tossed by a fierce wind.

"Are you doing that? Gabe, is this some kind of parlor trick?"

A sense of urgency throbbed through his veins. "Out," he ordered.

"What?"

"Move!" He reached for her, spinning her around toward the door.

"Stop it." She dug her heels into the carpet, resisting his efforts to propel her forward.

As he struggled with her the noise and movement from above grew more violent still. Emotions suddenly flew at him. Loneliness. Desperation. Despair. The same emotions he'd keyed into when he'd first arrived at the mansion.

"We have to get out now!" he shouted, fighting a wave of dizziness.

"You're scaring me!" She twisted her head around to look at him. Shocked disbelief made her eyes widen unnaturally.

He let go of her shoulders and grabbed her around the waist. Before she could utter more than a startled protest, he lifted her off her feet and rushed toward the door.

"*No!*" She pulled at his hands, trying to free herself.

The door slammed shut, barring their exit.

He skidded to a halt, loosening his grip on Angie until her feet touched the floor. For a fraction of a second, his mind refused to accept this bizarre occurrence.

"Gabe?"

He glanced down to find her staring up at him in frightened astonishment.

She twisted around in his embrace. "What's going on?"

"I don't know."

He held her to him tightly, almost afraid to let go. Then he remembered that under his fingers was tender human flesh. His hands went slack. He released her.

"I don't understand any of this," she said in a small, frightened voice as she rubbed her hands up and down her arms.

"Neither do I," he answered grimly.

He tried the brass doorknob. It didn't surprise him to discover it wouldn't budge, not even an inch. Frustrated, he threw his weight against the solid door. His only reward was a shooting pain down the right side of his body.

Then came the sound of an explosion.

Angie gasped.

An oath ripped from Gabriel's throat.

Later, he would barely remember that first explosion. What he would always remember was the way Angie looked: face drained of all color, eyes wide with bewilderment. What he would always remember was reaching for her, and how she clung to him as though he were the only thing standing between her and unknown terrors.

Holding her close, protectively, Gabriel watched, transfixed by the incredible sight of 40-watt bulbs exploding one by one, without breaking the glass globes surrounding them.

Mere seconds before the room was plunged into darkness, he was startled by a glimpse of movement he caught out of the corner of his eye. His gaze flew around the chamber, and in the rococo gilt mirror above the vanity table, he thought he saw someone.

A woman.

He stared, open-mouthed. Though he couldn't see the apparition clearly, he could feel her presence, as surely as he could smell rose water invading every fiber of his being.

"My God," he whispered. "Are you real?"

As though in response, the image in the mirror became more defined. He saw glimpses of pale skin and black hair piled high above an exquisite young face. She wore a light-colored gown, buttoned high at the throat and with lace and tiny pearl buttons down the front. He could not determine the color of her eyes, but he could not fail to see how heartbreakingly sad they seemed.

The last light went out, taking the mirror image with it.

And the room no longer smelled of roses.

Julia's moment of victory turned to anguish. It had not been her intention to frighten them so.

No one knew better than she what a hungry demon fear could be, for Charles had allowed fear to be her only companion.

She prayed with each breath that God would forgive her impatience.

❖ ————————— ❖

Seeing is believing. Seeing is damn well believing.

Gabriel kept repeating that to himself as he walked from one end of the kitchen to the other, then back again. Adrenaline pumped through his veins faster than the water he'd dumped into the automatic coffee maker.

Science had been tossed aside the moment he'd seen the entity in the mirror. It hadn't been an elaborate ruse. He was certain of it.

The Shadow Lady was real! He didn't need technology to confirm the sighting.

Never had he experienced anything like the phenomena he had witnessed that night. The whole thing was strange and a little frightening—and exhilarating! He felt as though he'd stepped out of reality and into . . . into heaven knew what.

He glanced at Angie and his enthusiasm waned.

She sat at the table, her head bowed, her face in her hands. At least she'd stopped shaking.

Gabriel didn't know what to say to her yet, which made him feel inadequate and helpless. He tucked his hands in his pockets and kept pacing as his thoughts turned to what had happened after the last light bulb exploded.

He had immediately hustled Angie out of the bedroom. Neither of them had paused to express surprise that the door had easily opened. Out in the hallway, she had spoken the only word that had passed between them since the incident. "Miles," she'd whispered hoarsely. They'd checked on the boy, finding him safe and sleeping soundly.

Then they'd come downstairs, Angie switching on every light they'd passed, as though needing the bright reassurance. Gabriel had settled her in a chair at the kitchen table with a lap blanket around her shoulders that he'd snatched from the back of a small settee in the foyer.

He shot another glance at her. It was ironic that he hadn't noticed until now the pattern of the blanket he'd thrown around her. Woven upon a background white as virgin snow were blood-red roses.

Talk about spooky coincidences.

The flower he had always associated with Valentine's Day and romance was taking on a different meaning. The next time he sent a woman flowers, he decided, they damn well wouldn't be roses.

He felt something bump against his leg and glanced down. Sugar Booger, who was pacing alongside him, grumbled and butted him again. Gabriel paused long enough to bend down and pet the feline's back.

Animals were quick to pick up on human emotions, and Sugar Booger, despite his indolent nature, was no exception. Gabriel wasn't sure, however, if the cat was attempting to comfort him or wanted comforting himself.

Sick of waiting for the brewing process to finish, he turned and strode over to the counter, where the coffee maker hissed and gurgled. Unceremoniously, he grabbed the handle of the pot, not caring in the least that the infernally slow appliance spat a thin stream of liquid down on the heating unit as he poured out two cups.

"Coffee's ready," he announced, carrying the cups to the table. "It's decaf."

He knew it sounded rather inane, but a little inane conversation was what they both needed while they sorted out in their minds what they had witnessed in Angie's room.

"Thanks." She straightened and accepted the cup.

"I laced it with brandy I looted from Miss Ivy's pantry."

The blanket had slipped on one side. He drew it up and settled it more securely around her. "You okay?"

She smiled. It was rather wan, but it was still a smile.

He squeezed her shoulder, then sat in the chair across from her. "Your aunt certainly keeps her pantry well stocked. Most of the time, one would be hard pressed to find more than a few cans of soup and a box of crackers in mine."

"Ivy likes to keep her guests well fed." She raised the cup with both hands and took a small sip. "I apologize for being such a rag-mannered hostess. You're a guest. I should be taking care of you."

She was accustomed to taking care of others, Gabriel thought. But who took care of her? He had the dispirited notion that the answer was no one.

"Don't worry about it." He ran a critical eye over her face. "You're still parchment-white."

"No sugar, Sherlock," she responded dryly.

"You take sugar in your coffee? Sorry. Stay put. I'll get it for you."

She laughed and waved him back down into his chair. "I didn't mean I wanted sugar. Jeez, you take things as literally as Miles does. I was using it as a substitute for the *S* word."

He grinned.

Angie found herself grinning back.

Strangely, she felt herself relaxing. After what she'd been through, she marveled that she could relax. How odd it was to feel content to be there in the middle of the night, wrapped in a blanket, alone in the kitchen with a man she'd known for such a short time. It didn't matter that she'd known him briefly when they were kids; he was still a stranger she didn't begin to know.

Angie had always taken pride that she could fend for herself and anyone else she chose to take to heart. But right now it felt good being pampered and protected. It seemed an undeserved luxury.

Suddenly, dark, frightening thoughts crept out from the shadows in her mind. *No!* She wasn't ready to deal with her questions and fears yet.

"I . . . uh, I developed the habit of saying 'sugar' and 'fudge' and all manner of the most ridiculous euphemisms when Miles was a baby," she said, forcing herself to think of ordinary things, pleasant things.

"Was he a precocious tyke?" The tone of his voice was kind, as kind as the smile he gave her.

She shuddered suddenly, and wondered if it had been caused by the sweetness of his smile or by the dark thoughts still struggling to be set free.

She lifted her cup and drank half its contents. After a moment, she said, "Miles started talking when he was barely five and a half months old. He bypassed the usual 'mama' and 'dada' stage."

"Somehow that doesn't surprise me."

"Of course, he never got the chance to call anyone dada. Miles was two months old when Jon died." She lifted a hand to run her fingers through her tousled hair.

"What was his first word?" Gabriel asked encouragingly.

"One morning at breakfast he surprised the heck out of me by pointing to something outside the window and saying quite clearly, 'What is that?' He followed it up with, 'Good cinnamon toast.' "

"I'm surprised his first word wasn't *spider*." Amusement lit up Gabriel's eyes.

"The thing he saw out the window probably was a spider."

Gabriel laughed, and she laughed with him. For a moment she savored the pleasurable feeling of companionship. She'd missed sharing with a man something so simple as laughter in the wee hours of the morning.

She leaned back, stretching her legs out. Her foot bumped into one of his. Neither of them moved away. The slight physical contact was . . . nice. Definitely nice.

"When did Miles acquire his interest in spiders?" he asked, rubbing his toe along the side of her bare foot. It took great effort on her part not to purr in delight.

"I'm not really certain. I remember one time . . ." The vivid memory swept through her mind's eye, and she smiled. "He wasn't quite three, I think. I had dressed him for church in a little suit with short pants and white knee socks. I thought he looked adorable. He claimed he looked silly.

"Anyway, while I was getting dressed, he slipped out and walked down to Aunt Clover's house—a block away. He crawled up under her front porch. I found out afterward that he'd gone to look at the giant spider's web he'd discovered there the day before."

"You must have been terribly frightened when you couldn't find him."

She nodded. "I was scared to death that someone had taken him. My aunts, my parents, Nila, and I looked for him for hours before Clover thought of looking under her back porch. The day before he had crawled under there to play while she was weeding her flower bed. Sure enough, we found him there. Asleep. It was muddy because it had rained early that morning. His suit was completely ruined, but I didn't care. I was so relieved to find him safe that all I could do was hug and kiss him."

Angie hid her face in her hand. "I'm babbling. Stop me before I embarrass myself by reciting my son's entire history, in excruciating detail."

"You're entitled to a little babbling. You've had a rough night."

His dark velvet voice was soothing to her jangled nerves. She felt the brief touch of his fingers upon her hand.

"Are you okay?"

Angie uncovered her face and glanced at him. She tried to smile, but couldn't.

Suddenly, she felt like weeping. Moisture gathered in her eyes and she fought to control it, succeeding only with great effort.

Her reaction didn't have a thing to do with the tender way Gabriel was looking at her, she told herself. She was just experiencing an emotional backlash.

"I'm okay. But for a while there I felt like I had been sucked into a black void."

"That's understandable," he murmured.

"It's the same feeling I had when Jon died. Numb disbelief, confusion, denial." She bowed her head. "The future I had taken for granted was gone. We'd just had a baby. We had so much living and loving to do."

"I'm sorry."

She forced back the need to cry. "Now, that black hole is filled with the same emotions. Only this time, I can't accept what I saw. I keep telling myself there has to be a rational explanation for what happened."

She lifted her gaze to meet his. "There is, isn't there? I mean, light bulbs do not explode like that for no reason."

Gabriel was hesitant to spill out everything he'd felt and seen. He sensed she needed to talk through all the rational explanations before she'd be able to accept something she was sure to consider irrational. It wasn't going to be easy for her to let go of the way she'd always perceived life and death to be. It wasn't easy for him, though the events that had occurred excited his scientist's curiosity.

"The light fixture could have been rigged," he said, staring thoughtfully into the steaming liquid in his cup.

"How? And shouldn't the glass globes have exploded when the light bulbs did?"

"Anyone with electrical know-how could have increased the voltage going into the chandelier. A surge of power would be enough to shatter the bulbs without breaking the surrounding globes."

He glanced up to find himself impaled by her steady gaze. All her nervousness had slipped back inside her to hold her in a tight grip. She chewed on her lower lip as she considered what he'd told her.

"Did you do it?" she blurted out. "I'm sorry, Gabe, but I have to know."

He jerked in surprise. Icy fingers of hurt and anger took hold of him. It didn't matter that it was a logical question, one the objective scientist in him would have asked in her place. In fact, he reminded himself, until there was conclusive evidence to the contrary, he ought to be asking that same thing of her.

"If I were capable of such an unscrupulous act, would

I admit it?" Go easy, he told himself. Remember, she's distraught.

The niggling doubt he saw in her eyes, though, was a knife in his heart. Dammit, he was sick to death of constantly having to prove his integrity to every Tom, Dick, and skeptic.

For once he wanted someone to believe in him. Not just someone, he amended. He wanted *her* to believe in him. Okay, so maybe that would be asking for a leap of blind faith on too short an acquaintance. But he couldn't help wanting it, even if the desire was based on pure emotion instead of intellect.

A laugh escaped her, one without humor. "I guess that was a stupid question."

"Not at all."

He strived to control his rising anger, to control his tone of voice. It didn't work. He gave her a cool, hard stare. "I could ask you the same question."

"Gabe!" She recoiled as though he'd struck her.

He felt sick, but he couldn't stop. "You could be putting on an act about not wanting me here. It's possible *you* rigged the chandelier and the door to convince me something paranormal is going on here."

"That's ridiculous!" She stood up so abruptly, the blanket slid from her shoulders and her chair almost tipped backward. She ignored both and stood glaring down at him.

"No it isn't. Unscrupulous people have tried to fool me before."

She stepped backward. "How *dare* you."

He got up and walked around the table.

"Make it easy on both of us, Angie. Confess this whole thing is a hoax. What do you hope to gain by it? Publicity for the Kingston Inn?"

"That accusation is untrue and insulting." She pinned him with a haughty look, making him remember what it had felt like to be the clumsy Geek squirming under the Beauty's cool stare.

"Is it?" He raised his eyebrows, giving her a taste of her own disdain. "Should I accept that you're telling the truth simply because you say so?"

"Yes!" She turned her back as though dismissing him, rejecting him.

"Some people love the idea of staying in a haunted house," he said. "You're shrewd enough to realize the value of a few newspaper articles speculating on the ghost who haunts the old Kingston mansion."

Her back stiffened. He heard the sharp intake of her breath.

Okay, he thought. Enough of this. He knew he was hurting her. But he couldn't seem to stop his words, any more than he could stem the emotions rushing through him like raging floodwaters. "The public would line up at the door for a chance to see the Shadow Lady. You could fill this place to the rafters with guests for a solid year."

"Go to hell." Angie stormed toward the counter, where she'd left her cigarettes and lighter.

She didn't know he could move so fast or look so

furious. Her mouth fell open in surprise as he spun her around and backed her up against the door of the stainless-steel refrigerator.

"It hurts to be called a liar, doesn't it?" he said softly.

She didn't know he could look so cold. His eyes, bright with anger, glistened like a thin surface of ice over a lake in winter.

Strangely, she hadn't considered that he might have a temper, but now that it was staring her in the face, she found she wasn't surprised. She should have guessed that his intensity extended to all his emotions, from curiosity to passion to anger.

"You should be careful how quickly you judge"—his voice went even softer, causing a chill to creep up her spine—"unless you're willing to accept a few unpleasant judgments yourself."

Gabriel's gaze raked her pale face, which was now stained by a touch of crimson. She wasn't afraid, but her breathing was ragged and her eyes were blazing.

Common sense told him his point had been made and he should now back off. But she closed her eyes, and he felt as though a door were being shut in his face. "I didn't tamper with the chandelier," he said, pushing to keep that door from closing.

"Well, neither did I!"

He didn't mind suddenly finding himself on the receiving end of a resentful stare. At least now she wasn't dismissing him or shutting him out.

He framed her face with his hands. "I didn't really think you did."

A look of anguish glazed her eyes. He sensed the wave of grief that swept over her. She opened her mouth to speak, but no sound emerged. She cleared her throat and stammered, "Mi—Mi—Miles. You don't think—" Her breath hitched and she looked scared. "You don't think *he* did it. He couldn't have—"

"No!" he quickly interrupted, placing his fingers on her lips to stop the flow of grief-stricken words. "I am certain he had nothing to do with what happened. I *know* he didn't."

He felt the tension begin to seep from her body at the conviction in his voice. "Please forget I suggested Miles could unknowingly be the cause of anything happening here. I was just trying hard not to let my personal feelings cloud my professional judgment."

Angie closed her eyes and slumped against the smooth metal at her back. After a moment, she opened her eyes and whispered, "Thank you for that. Deep down inside I was afraid there might be some truth in what you said about him repressing his emotions. I was so afraid."

"I know. I'm sorry."

"I honestly didn't think you were responsible for what happened," she said in a small voice. "I was just . . ."

"Grasping for a plausible explanation," he supplied for her.

"Yes. I'm sorry."

They stood looking at one another, and for a time

each was content with forgiving, content just to hold each other in sight.

"What was it like growing up psychic?" she asked, splaying the fingers of one hand over his chest, taking comfort in the solid feel of his body.

"Harrowing . . . bewildering. Imagine an overload of sensory information, sensations so powerful you suffer nausea or dizziness, even physical pain."

He spoke without bitterness or self-pity. Whatever his childhood trials had been, she didn't think he was affected by them now. Still, she could not help feeling a wave of compassion for the boy who'd experienced heaven only knew what.

"Don't do that, Angie. Please."

A large, fat tear rolled down her cheek, falling with a splash, bursting like a child's balloon. "I didn't mean to get weepy on you. Believe it or not, I usually only cry over sappy movies and corny TV commercials about mothers and babies and such."

He swiped at a second tear with his thumb. "Don't be sad. I can't think straight when you're sad." He smiled at her with such sweetness, it drew a third tear from her.

He brushed her cheek with the palm of his hand, then threaded his fingers in her hair. "I go halfway to heaven touching you." His voice, his gaze were so passionate, her heart began to beat wildly.

Helplessly, so softly she doubted he could hear, she whispered, "So could I."

Unable to handle one more intense emotion, she got

hold of herself and turned off the waterworks. "First thing in the morning, I'm going to call an electrician to check that damn light fixture."

"I think you should," he agreed mildly. "I would have suggested that course of action myself. However, I have a feeling the electrician won't be able to supply the rational explanation you want."

"I don't like this, Gabriel. Tell me we're both just having the same nightmare."

"You don't like liars," he reminded her gently.

"It wouldn't hurt, just this once."

"We're awake. What happened was real." As he spoke, he tilted her chin up, forcing her eyes to meet his. "I dreamed something was going to happen in your room. Something involving the light fixture. I knew it had to do with the entity because of the rosewater scent. It was the same fragrance I smelled in the foyer yesterday, just before I sensed the presence of the entity."

"What?" she cried out, her heart scampering wildly, her hands grasping at his shoulders.

NINE

Gabriel closed his eyes. "It was the day I arrived. You didn't want me to stay here. I was trying to leave, but the front door wouldn't open. I smelled rose water so strong it almost made me ill. I felt the entity's presence. Then you spoke to me and the feeling—the entity—was gone."

Silence, then, "Gabe, why didn't you say something about it to me then?"

"Would you have believed me if I had?" He opened his eyes, his gaze searching her face.

"No." She gave him a rueful smile.

"I *saw* her tonight."

"Who?"

"The ghost. I saw her in your vanity mirror just before the last light bulb exploded."

Angie paled and shook her head in denial. It wasn't possible! He couldn't have seen what he'd thought. It was crazy. And yet—

In the brightly lit kitchen, she studied his face. Everything about him shouted honest, levelheaded, trustworthy. As much as she wished she could deny it, she believed he truly thought he had seen a ghost.

Perversely, she tried one last time to make sense of something that didn't make sense at all. "I don't doubt you saw something, Gabe. But maybe it was my reflection you saw. You know how the mind can play tricks in stressful situations."

Amusement curved his lips. "It wasn't your reflection."

"Are you sure?"

He stopped touching her. His arms fell to his sides as he stepped backward. "It wasn't you. I saw a shadowy figure take shape in the mirror. It was a woman. Her hair was black and it was piled loosely on top of her head. She had on one of those old-fashioned gowns, high at the neck and with rows of tiny pearl buttons down the front."

Angie didn't know what to think. She didn't doubt he'd seen something. But a ghost? The rational part of her mind rebelled.

He smiled sadly at her silence. "You think I'm crazy?"

She hesitated, gnawing her lip. "Gabriel . . ."

"Go ahead. Call me crazy." He moved closer again, bringing his lean body into contact with hers. She shivered, not from fear but from the jolt of sensual awareness spreading through her.

"I don't think you're crazy."

"But you do think it was just my imagination working overtime," he challenged softly, placing his hands on the refrigerator, one of each side of her head.

Angie felt emotionally as well as physically trapped. After a long moment of silence, she let out an unsteady breath. "I—I can't. I don't know what to think right now."

It obviously wasn't the answer he had hoped to hear. His incredible eyes were filled with wistfulness. He stepped back again and turned away.

"I'm sorry, Gabriel. I don't know what you saw. But I don't want to believe it was a ghost. And I'm too confused to think about it anymore."

He faced her. His eyes had emptied of any discernible emotion. "I didn't believe in ghosts either."

"What do you mean you didn't believe in them?" she asked incredulously. "You're a ghostbuster."

"I had an open mind on the subject of the existence of apparitions, but I didn't *believe* in them."

"I don't understand."

"I regard *belief* as something appropriate in matters of religion or love. Belief requires a certain leap of blind faith. As a scientist—"

"You don't take leaps of blind faith," she finished for him.

"Never with my subject matter. I study evidence. Until tonight, I'd never seen a ghost."

Had he claimed he believed in ghosts with all his

heart and soul and that he'd seen a hundred spooks before, Angie might have been able to hang on to her doubts. Fortunately, he didn't press the matter any further.

"Speaking of evidence," he said, "I should check the equipment. Will you be all right by yourself?"

If there really was a ghost, she didn't want him to go. "Couldn't we . . . I'd rather you stay here, just a little longer."

What was she doing, sounding like a frightened child? She didn't want him to think she was the wimpy type that jumped at shadows.

"No, it's okay," she said, starting to move away. "Go on. I'll be fine."

He stopped her with a hand on her shoulder. "It's all right. I don't have to check the equipment now. Whatever it recorded will still be there in an hour or in the morning. Go sit down. I'll warm up our coffee and we can talk for a while."

"Thank you."

He turned away.

"Gabe . . . I mean, Gabriel."

He glanced back at her.

"I really want to say *thanks*. You've been very . . . sweet to me tonight."

He was looking at her in the same open way as he had in the restaurant—with naked longing, sexuality, desire, a lifetime of loneliness. It was an expression she could not see without her heart twisting in all directions.

Suddenly her thoughts and feelings couldn't translate into words. Nothing seemed to exist beyond her need to have him close to her, to touch him, to have him touch her.

She wants to touch me. Gabriel could feel it. The impression was so strong, it made him breathless. He could feel the part of her that was reaching out, full of wanting, but knowing she should be cautious.

The air was thick with feelings, different ones now that had nothing to do with ghosts. And he knew there wasn't a thing either of them could do about them anymore.

His heart was in his smile. Gabriel could feel that, too, as he poured them both another cup of coffee. In mutual silent consent, they carried their cups and the rose blanket into the cozy den off the kitchen.

Instead of turning on the lights, Angie walked over to the fireplace. Gabriel dropped the blanket on the sofa and watched as she lit the candles that were on the mantel. Tiny flames sprang to life, and she was bathed in flickering golden ribbons that reflected in her eyes as she crossed the room to place the candles on the glass-topped wicker trunk in front of the sofa.

She stretched her arm toward him. "Remember what you said to me in the restaurant about reaching for your hand? I'm reaching, Gabe."

Her voice had a dreamy quality that stirred him, and he lowered his voice to match the mood it created. "It's yours. Whenever, however, you want."

He raised her hand to his lips, pressing a kiss upon the tips of her fingers. The warmth of her fingers spreading over his lower lip had an immediate effect on his senses. She was like a beautiful luxury, exotically fragrant, all silk and ivory and gold, richly inviting, deeply desirable.

"This is courtship, uh?" he said, managing a shaky smile.

"It's . . . an unusual one." Her breath wavered on a sigh. She withdrew her hand from his grasp and held it over her heart, then lifted it to her mouth as though savoring the kiss she wished he had placed there instead. She lowered her arm to her side and was still for a moment.

A sudden smile swept over her face. "Sometimes, when I look at you, nothing else exists, I feel like we're alone in the universe."

"I think we are."

Angie felt waves of unexpected shyness. Her conscience whispered that she should behave cautiously with him, but she found it difficult to listen. She was so full of feelings for him, feelings that were dancing on every nerve ending in her body.

The hell with caution, she thought. She moved closer to touch her lips to his, stroking his mouth tenderly, learning all over again the shape, the unique textures and contours, the ebb and flow of his breath. Slowly, she increased the contact until his mouth came alive and his arms went around her.

His body shifted closer, and pleasure sparked in all the places in her body where they touched. His chest made a caressing movement against her breasts. The faint erotic pressure of his hips and thighs against hers reminded her of the powerful pull of desire that had been simmering between them since he'd walked into her life.

Moaning, Gabriel drew her to him. He deepened the kiss with something close to panic, needing the warm assurance that her passion was real. And that it was his. All his.

Her tongue tangled with his, desire and intimacy merging blindly, struggling for more. He could feel her breasts yield against him, her hands run demandingly over his back. She made him feel he had passed beyond the boundaries of human joy.

He moved his mouth over her face, her throat. She made some sound, a long, slow sigh, that made his pulse hammer. Lord, she was sweet.

When he placed a hand over the silk covering her breast, Angie arched her back. An aching fullness sprang to life inside her. The tips of his fingers brushed over one nipple, steeping her in mindless pleasure. Her body and mind knew only sensations as his lips replaced his fingers at her breasts.

It was so easy. She should have known it would be this easy to lose herself in him.

"Gabe . . ." His name came on a sigh.

Lifting his head, he cradled her face in his hands. He

tried to read every nuance of her beautiful eyes, hoping to see that she wanted to make love with him as much as he wanted to love her.

"Yes?" he whispered.

She gazed back at him for a long moment. "No," she said at last with breathless regret. Her hands smoothed over his naked chest, making him feel dizzy and breathless too. "Not yet. Not tonight."

Again he felt the wistful part of her as her soft and gentle hands made yearning motions over his skin, wanting to reach out to be a part of him. His capacity to understand her was becoming greater. He understood that she needed time to sort out what was in her heart and mind. He understood, as did she, how close they were to breaking all inhibitions, how close they were to surrendering to the need to be together.

He heard her words in his mind, and felt their longing, before she spoke them. "But soon, Gabe. Very soon."

Even as he savored her promise, he felt shaken. His psychic and emotional link with her was stronger than anything he'd ever felt before.

Gabriel had never dared to hope he would feel so intimately connected to another person. In varying degrees, he'd felt a separateness from the rest of the human race all his twenty-eight years. Now, because of her, that separateness was passing from him.

Again by some silent mutual consent, they arranged

themselves on the sofa and spread the blanket over them both. She tucked her legs beneath her and nestled against him, a light sensual weight on the right side of his torso.

The silence was comfortable. Their coffee grew cold in the cups on the wicker trunk. Holding each other was everything and it was unlike anything Gabriel had ever experienced before. For now, it was enough.

Her hair teased his cheek and shoulder as she turned her face toward him. He lifted his head. Close above her, he saw concern in her face.

"Gabe, do you think she was trying to hurt us?"

He didn't have to ask who she meant. Nor did he need to ask if she was now convinced, as he was, that the entity was real.

Something whispered inside his soul, telling him that Angie's acceptance of the apparition's existence was bringing her closer to accepting who and what Gabriel Richards was. Without realizing it, she had just given him a gift that could not be placed in a box and wrapped with pretty paper and ribbons, a priceless gift beyond compare.

"I've been pondering and exploring that question in my mind," he told her.

She smiled a little. "Most people would have said they had been 'thinking' about it."

"Isn't it the same thing?"

The smile grew. "No. It's a matter of depth. You 'ponder and explore,' seeking answers for things beyond our limited human understanding. You're unique, Gabe. More unique than anyone I've ever known."

He gave her an amused look. "So I fit right in with your eccentric relatives?"

She laughed. It was a sound that delighted him, a sound more beautiful and clear than the peal of silver bells ringing out a Christmas carol.

"My family is wonderfully weird," Angie said. "*You* are wonderfully unique in a way that isn't the least bit weird or eccentric." She watched the lines and planes of his face become supple and smile-softened. "Now tell me what you've been pondering."

"I'm positive the apparition did not mean to harm us." He shifted one hand to the side of her face, his thumb lightly following the crescent of her cheekbone. In that touch there was more tenderness, more sweetness than she had ever imagined was possible.

"But you dreamed I was in danger," she reminded him, frowning.

He skimmed his fingertips over the outer rim of her ear as he answered. "It was a misinterpretation on my part. You've been fighting against having me here, and the Shadow Lady knows that. I think the phenomenon we experienced was simply her way of attracting attention, her way of letting both of us know she is here, and that she is real."

"She got my attention, all right. In a very rude manner, I might add."

He smiled briefly, then said, "I've also been considering the dream you had tonight." He drew his fingers through her hair. "Angie, you experienced what we call a psychic realistic dream."

She quickly straightened. As she turned an indignant look upon him, strands of her hair slipped through his fingers like wispy silk threads. "Do you mean to tell me that sneaky ghost invaded the privacy of my mind and put images in my head?"

He looked as though he was suppressing a laugh. "Think of it as a psychic transmission. Without being consciously aware of it, you received sensory information that resulted in the events you dreamed about."

"I don't like it. But you may be right." She was thoughtful for a moment. "I know I was there in that old garden for an unknown purpose. But what puzzles me is that the area did not look like it does now. I had a feeling I was seeing it as it might have been originally, a beautiful and lovingly tended garden, a place for quiet reflection."

"It could be that you were seeing it as the entity remembers it. How fascinating!"

"It's downright scary, Gabriel Richards."

"It's downright amazing."

"You can be awed and amazed all you like," she told him tartly. "I don't want to be seeing anything through a ghost's eyes. And the only person I want rooting around my subconscious mind is me." She paused. "Or a psychiatrist. A *living* one."

"What significance does that particular place have for

the entity?" he asked, puzzling aloud. "She wanted you to go there. She wanted you to see the garden in a particular way. It *must* be important."

"Maybe she died there."

"I don't know how I know—so don't ask—but I think that whatever happened to her happened here in the house. This is where she repeatedly makes her appearance."

She eyed him speculatively. "Can't you ask the ghost to send you some kind of message clairvoyantly or something?"

Gabriel shook his head. "There are some psychics who have such strong abilities that they probably could do that. Unfortunately, I'm not one of them. I hate to tell you this, but I have never been able to command my clairvoyant ability at will. It comes and goes as it pleases. If you lost your car keys, I couldn't just close my eyes and conjure up a mental picture of where they were."

"Then what good is having such an ability if you can't use it when you want to?"

"It's had a few good uses over the years." He thought of the time he'd stopped his parents from boarding a private airplane. It had taken off without them, and it had crashed, as he had foreseen. The pilot and two passengers, who had disregarded his warning, had sustained serious injuries.

"Well, hell," Angie muttered. "Then there's a chance that this thing could drag on forever."

"It's a distinct possibility that we may never know

who the Shadow Lady is and why she is bound to this place." His brow wrinkled. "That would make Miss Ivy rather unhappy. For some reason, she and Miles both think I can perform some kind of spiritual rescue."

"Oh, good grief. That sounds just like Ivy."

All of a sudden she groaned and dropped her face into her palm.

"What's wrong?"

"I just remembered some scenes from *The Exorcist*." She glanced up and frowned at him. "If you get possessed by that sneaky ghost, and you start talking in a funny voice, and your head begins spinning around, I'm out of here. History. Gone. Do you hear me?"

Gabriel couldn't resist. He allowed his face to go slack, his eyes to roll up, and his head to fall back. Tossing his head from side to side, he began to moan and speak gibberish in a harsh, guttural tone.

She jabbed an elbow into his ribs. "Put a cork in it, Gabe. I am not amused."

He looked down at her. "Yes you are. You're smiling."

"Just a little." She added teasingly, "You've got a sick sense of humor, but at least you have one."

"Gee, thanks," he said dryly, wrapping his arms around her.

Angie sank against him. For a while she simply enjoyed the comfortable feel of his arms and a quiet companionship that was as warm as the blanket covering them both.

Then she began trying to recall all the details of her dream, in hopes of coming up with some clue as to why the garden might be important. When she could not uncover any answers, her mind turned to the dream lover. Was he real, or simply a fantasy?

She remembered that she hadn't told Gabriel about the man who had been with her in the garden. Perhaps she shouldn't have left out that detail. It could have some significance too.

"Gabe, there's something I didn't mention to you about my dream."

"Oh?"

She chewed on her lower lip, then said hesitantly, "I wasn't alone. Someone was with me."

"Do you know who it was?"

Her thoughts turned inward. Slowly, a vague form began to take shape in her mind. She compared the simple pleasure and joy she'd felt when the dream lover had been beside her, holding her hand, with the flesh-and-blood reality of the way she'd felt when Gabriel had held her hand a little while ago. Could it be . . . ?

In a shaky voice, she asked, "Is it possible—" She started over. "These psychic realistic dreams—do they foreshadow events to come?" Her breath got trapped in her throat as she waited for him to speak.

"We have reason to think such dreams can be a realistic representation of an event to come or an event that is actually happening at the time of the dream. Why do you ask?"

"Hold my hand."

"Why?"

"Please."

He did as she asked, and she had no doubt it was the hand of her dream lover. The knowledge exploded inside her mind, filling her with a thousand fragmented thoughts and emotions.

The joyous feeling of being in love seeped into her every pore. Angie stared at the flickering candle flames.

She was in love with him. It was just as simple—just as easy—as that.

Love. She had feared she would never be blessed with that miracle again.

Angie was suddenly overwhelmed with emotions. She wanted to be with him, to find out everything about him, to know him in all his various moods. She wanted to know what made him laugh, what made him sad, what made his eyes glow with passion. She wanted to spend quiet evenings with him and share wildly passionate nights. She wanted a lifetime of greeting him at the door with, "Hi, darling, how was your day?" as he came home from work.

Gabriel held himself very still as he was hit hard by an emotional overload that caused him to feel disoriented and dizzy. They were her emotions, not his. He sensed something evolving inside her, something taking on shape, color, and life. A hazy image of Angie smiling at him from a doorway formed in his mind.

The image faded as her emotions smoothed out like a

sea after a storm, leaving her tranquil and him totally confused. After a few seconds, his dizziness and disorientation subsided, and he let out the breath he had not been aware of holding.

"It was you, Gabe," she said in that purring, sensual voice that never failed to root around some ticklish place in his brain. "It was you. *You* were with me."

"Angie?"

"Just hold me, please." She snuggled against him. "I'm so tired. I can't think anymore tonight."

He complied without questioning her further. But he wondered why he had been a part of her dream, wondered what it might mean.

Long after her breathing slowed with sleep, he held her close, her head nestled against his shoulder. He listened to the profound quietude, watching with pleasure how the candlelight threw delicate shadows across her body.

A feeling of being watched awakened Gabriel the next morning.

Bright light poured into the room through the windows, hurting his eyes. It took him a second or two to focus properly, as well as to remember where he was and that the warm weight pressing against him was Angie.

A slow, lazy smile curved his mouth. He breathed in deeply and hugged Angie's sleeping body before glancing around.

Miles sat Indian fashion on the floor, his elbows resting on his knees, his face cradled between his hands, his myopic gaze glued to Gabriel's face. Sugar Booger cat was lounging beside him and seemed to be staring curiously too.

"Good morning, Miles."

"Good morning, sir. Why are you cuddling my mother? Is she sick?"

"She's just sleeping."

Comprehension replaced curiosity in the boy's eyes. "Oh, I see. You like each other," he said with a wise little nod. And damned if it didn't look to Gabriel like the cat nodded sagely too.

"Ah, yes. We do like each other."

"Jake cuddles Nila. They're having a baby, you know."

Gabriel felt a rise of panic. *Lord, don't let this lead to a birds-and-bees session. I'm not prepared for this.*

"Jake married Nila. Are you going to marry my mother?"

"I don't know, Miles." All the persistent courting in the world wouldn't do a bit of good if Angie didn't love him or want to marry him. That was not a happy thought to wake up to.

Gabriel also knew that Miles's feelings would be an important part of any marriage equation for Angie. "How would you feel about your mother marrying me? That is, if she wanted to be my wife."

Miles puckered his brow and twisted his mouth sideways as he thought that over. "I wouldn't mind, though it would seem strange at first. But I like you. You *do* know a great deal about spiders. So I suppose we would get along famously."

Gabriel smiled. He'd come there to hunt a ghost. What were the chances he would take home a family? Husband and father. Whoa! It boggled the mind.

Miles scooped up the cat and stood. "By the way, did your cameras and equipment pick up any trace of the Shadow Lady last night?"

"I don't know. I haven't monitored what was recorded yet." Excitement traveled through him. He couldn't wait to find out if he now had solid evidence that would prove the existence of apparitions.

"Oh. I thought you had." The boy gave him a puzzled look. "The cameras are covered with lace doilies. The recording equipment is switched off too. I didn't touch anything, honest," he added quickly. "I just looked."

Gabriel had started to ease himself away from Angie. The boy's words stopped him cold.

He hadn't touched the equipment. Angie had not left his side since they'd come downstairs last night. Nor did he think Miles had done it, deliberately or subconsciously. That left only one possibility.

The Shadow Lady had done it.

TEN

That afternoon found Angie once again sharing the den sofa with Gabriel. Miles and Sugar Booger were safely ensconced in the Madison household. An electrician had given the chandelier and electrical wiring a thorough going-over and had gone away scratching his head in puzzlement and murmuring, "Power surge. Gotta be a power surge."

Angie had been in a slight daze all day, thinking about Gabriel, about what had happened between them the night before, about their growing emotional and physical bond, about what would surely happen now that they were alone in the house.

Everything seemed to be moving and changing so fast. Perhaps too fast. Something deeper and more intimate came forth with each moment she spent with him, even quiet moments like now.

She glanced up for the tenth time from the material

she was supposed to be reading and settled her gaze upon Gabriel. Just looking at him, being near him, made her feel a lifting sensation in her chest.

So close. Yet so far away. He was only a few feet from her, slouched in the opposite corner of the sofa, but he might as well have been on another planet. It amazed her that a human being could sit so still for so long.

He hadn't altered his position the least bit in over half an hour. His arms were folded over his chest, his legs were stretched out, one athletic shoe-shod foot was crossed over the other, his sexy lower lip poked out just a little, his eyes stared straight ahead.

That morning she had dressed to match her romantic mood, in soft, feminine clothing and heart-shaped vintage jewelry. For all the notice he was taking of her, though, she could have saved herself the trouble and worn old jeans and a T-shirt, like him. Though she had to admit, he did look mighty fine in what he'd thrown together.

"Gabe?"

He didn't respond. Didn't even twitch so much as an eyelash. His ability to block out everything around him both impressed and irked her.

Well, she thought, she'd wanted to know him in all his various moods. He was not a happy ghostbuster today.

She stuffed papers back into the folder and closed it. Then she unbent one leg from beneath her and slowly inched her bare foot toward him. "Gabe!" she shouted at the same time as she goosed his thigh with her toes.

"Huh?"

"Are you pouting?"

He turned his head to meet her gaze. "Scientists *never* pout."

"Your lower lip is stuck out halfway to Richmond." She grinned. "You're pouting because your nifty toys let you down." Four times that day she had watched him patiently reset every piece of his electronic gadgets. Four times he'd returned to find them all out of commission.

"Those 'nifty toys,' as you call them, are highly sensitive pieces of modern electronic technology," he told her loftily.

She blew a raspberry to show him what she thought of that. "Perhaps a deck of tarot cards would be more useful after all."

"I hope the Shadow Lady gets you for that."

"Poor Gabe," she couldn't resist teasing. "Stuck with a camera-shy ghost."

"It's not funny."

She nodded. "Yes it is."

"Infidel. You must pay for your levity." He grinned mischievously as he grabbed her by the ankle.

"No tickling!" Laughing, she kicked and squirmed, but she couldn't avoid the nimble fingers dancing over the sensitive sole of her foot.

"Say 'poltergeist,' " he demanded in between tickling and laughing almost as hard as she was.

"Pol—pol—polter—geist."

"Louder. I can't hear you."

"POLTERGEIST!"

As he released her, she launched herself at him, raising the manila folder to smack him. He caught her wrists. Her skirt billowed, then drifted over his legs as he dragged her down onto his thighs.

She dropped the folder onto her lap and snuggled up against him with a contented sigh. "You're fun, Gabe."

He looked amused. "I don't believe anyone has ever called me 'fun' before."

"Well, I don't see why not." She looped an arm around his neck and gave him a saucy grin. "You're lots of fun. That is, when you're not pondering too much for your own good."

"I think you're good for me." He pressed a quick kiss to her lips and smoothed his hand back and forth over her midriff. Her body responded instantly with tingling pleasure.

Pulling back a fraction, he whispered, "You're smiling."

"How can you tell?" she whispered back, loving this unsuspected playful side of him. His body felt so good, so familiar, so full of promise.

"I felt it with my mouth."

"What does my smile feel like?"

"Like you're holding my heart in your hand."

Cradling the back of his head, she bought their lips together once more in a deeper kiss. She drove her fingers into his hair, clinging to the kiss until they were both shuddering and breathless.

She buried her face in the hollow of his throat. He tucked her closer with one hand, the other lovingly stroking her hair.

Gabriel closed his eyes to steady himself against an unsatisfiable hunger for more. The sweet seductive power of what was happening between them filled him with wonder and a longing so intense it was painful.

His fate was linked with hers. But for how long? he wondered. Four short weeks, or a lifetime? Thinking back on his conversation with Miles that morning, he fervently hoped for the latter: a wife and a son.

"Gabe?"

"What?"

"This is nice, isn't it?" Long, sensitive fingers caressed his neck, the motion inducing shivers up his spine.

"Yes," he breathed. Desire stung him with fresh insistence.

"Talk to me." Her voice compelled him like a caress. One bewitching finger dipped beneath his collar to trace a path back and forth.

"About what?"

"You. I want to know everything about you."

"That ought to fill up at least five minutes." He smiled ruefully.

"I doubt it. I've never met anything like you, so passionately interested in exploring the unknown. I would say you're an idealistic man. Kind. Affectionate. Sincere. Incredibly intuitive."

She raised her head, looked at him with beguiling eyes. "You have a complex, intricate mind that instantly absorbs and analyzes. I should think that would be difficult for you, because you must find yourself easily bored with those around you, who are almost never as quick or clever."

"An interesting analysis." She was more observant of human nature, more in tune with him than he'd thought. "Shall I describe you?"

She smiled a little. "All right."

"You are more clever than most people realize. You're smart, energetic, loyal. People have to earn your trust." He watched her smile widen. "Your beauty is magnetic and attracts admiration, attention. But it blinds some people, and that's all they see. I think that's caused you some trouble over the years." Her smile took on an ironic edge. "You look beyond physical beauty in others and it disappoints you when other people fail to look beyond yours."

"You do read emotions rather well, don't you?"

He smiled, but didn't comment on that. Reaching up, he ran the back of his hand down her velvet-smooth cheek. "When you love, you love unselfishly, with everything you are."

Love me like that, he wanted to say, but he couldn't. He'd never asked any woman for her love. He'd never wanted to before. Now that he did, he found it took more guts than he'd imagined.

In the silence that followed, Angie's thoughts were a quagmire, her senses as scattered as her wits. Her feelings for him were so new and fragile, so filled with gray areas of apprehension. She wished she had his gift for reading emotions in others. Perhaps then she would feel more confident about the outcome of their relationship.

What would happen to their fledgling relationship when his work there was done? Would he want to continue a long-distance romance? Could her heart cope with that? Would he want something more permanent? Did she want forever with him? Or was she just fooling herself and in love with the idea of being in love again?

"No frowning," he murmured, smoothing away the lines between her eyebrows. "No worrying about anything else today. Especially no worrying about us. We have so little time. Okay?"

So little time. Shaken, she asked, "Reading my mind again, are you?"

"No." His wonderful mouth quirked into a smile. "I read your body language. Let's get back to getting to know each other. When is your birthday?"

She shoved her concerns to the back of her mind and decided to simply enjoy being with him. For now. "November twenty-second. I'll be thirty for the second time. When is your birthday? How old will you be? Do you like birthday cakes with tons of gooey icing?"

"March first. Twenty-nine. Yes. White frosting. What's your favorite color?"

"Red. Yours?"

"The color of your eyes."

She looked at him, her heart beginning to beat quickly. He looked back, his gaze heated but full of that otherworldly patience he had. "Kiss me," she demanded unsteadily.

"As you wish." Gabriel captured her mouth in a kiss of devouring intimacy. Nothing seemed to exist for him beyond his need to have her body close to his and to have her kiss banish the chill of loneliness inside his soul.

When he released her, he stared down at her. "You have been a major disturbance since I first saw you. You fill me with desire by simply being in the same room." He moved his hand over her from hip to thigh and back again, learning the shape of her through the cotton skirt.

She laughed, softly, seductively. "I know the feeling."

He kissed her lips, her chin. "I love the shape and feel of you," he murmured, continuing to run his hand over her leg.

The folder lying on her lap got in the way of further exploration. As he absently picked it up, he raised his head to smile at her. He started to toss the folder aside, but some niggling feeling made him glance at it first. A single sheet of paper stuck partway out. It caught and held his attention, even though Angie was nibbling on his ear and working magic with her fingers in his hair. He placed the folder back on her lap and worked that one paper free.

It was a photocopy of an old newspaper article. The headline read: *Kingston Builds Honeymoon House for Bride.* A grainy black-and-white photograph showed a man and woman in front of the mansion-in-progress. The caption beneath the picture read: *Charles Kingston and his bride, Julia Rose Kingston, admiring the work on their new home.*

In some distant corner of his mind, he heard Angie sigh and felt her warm breath teasing his neck. Lord, she was wonderful.

He lifted the paper higher and peered closely at the woman in the photograph. His heartbeat suddenly quickened, partly because Angie was doing great things to his earlobe, and partly because he recognized the stunning beauty in the photo.

"Angie, you did it!"

She raised her head to look at him. "Did what?"

"The Shadow Lady." His voice rose in excitement. "You found her. Good work, babe." He smacked a kiss on her lips.

She laughed. "I'd pat myself on the back for being so clever, but I have no idea what you're talking about."

"Look at the woman in this photograph." He waved the sheet of paper in front of her face.

Angie took hold of his wrist. "Be still so I can see it. Mmmmm, lovely frock coat and hat she has on."

"Who cares about her clothes. Look—"

"*I* do. I love turn-of-the-century fashions."

"This is the woman I saw in your mirror last night."

That deflated Angie's playful mood and threw cold water on her libido. She took the paper from him and carefully studied the photo.

The woman was young, perhaps eighteen or twenty. There was a look of innocent simplicity, a lack of worldly wisdom, in her captivating heart-shaped face, which wasn't surprising given her age and the era she had lived in. She wore her dark hair swept up and almost hidden beneath her hat.

It was the young woman's dark eyes that truly captured Angie's interest. She thought she detected an expression in them that did not match the smile on Julia's face.

"Well?" Gabriel said impatiently.

"She's lovely." She met his gaze. "Are you sure this is the face you saw?"

"I'm absolutely certain. Her name is Julia *Rose* Kingston. What does that suggest to you?"

"With a maiden name like Rose," Angie said slowly, "it's possible her signature perfume could have been roses. Rose and sandalwood were two of the popular fragrances of her era."

"Bingo." He looked positively triumphant.

She moved to sit beside him and placed the folder on top of the wicker trunk. "I read this article a little while ago. Julia was a native of Danville. Charles Kingston is described as a wealthy entrepreneur who retired to this area from Richmond. Julia had been married to him for about two months when this photo was taken.

The house was his wedding present to her, along with some very expensive emerald and diamond jewelry that was described in great detail."

"Doesn't really tell us much about her personally," he remarked.

"Nope."

"What do you think of Charles Kingston?"

She lowered her gaze to the photocopy. The man stood very close to his young bride, one arm around her waist and his hand tucked possessively to her side. He appeared to be in his late fifties. Everything about him was big—not fat, but big as in powerful.

"I don't particularly find him handsome," she said thoughtfully. "His expression is a shade too self-satisfied. There's something about his sharp slash of a mouth that makes me think he's humorless, pretentious maybe."

Gabriel nodded. "I'm getting the same impression. For some reason, the man sets my teeth on edge."

"I wonder what attracted Julia to him. His money? Social position?"

"Perhaps we're assuming too much from this one photograph. For all we know Kingston might have been a charmer."

"That's true. Julia is smiling happily enough. I suppose she could have loved him very—"

Gabriel jerked convulsively and let out a grunt.

"Are you okay?" She put her hand on his shoulder.

His features were scrunched up as though he were in pain. His whole body was tense, and he was clutching his left side at the waist.

"Yeah," he breathed out. The tight muscles under her hand began to relax and his expression smoothed out in relief.

"What happened?"

He frowned. "For a moment I had a sharp pain in my side. It's weird, but it felt like fingers were pinching and digging into my skin."

Angie returned his frown. "Are you sure it wasn't a muscle spasm or something like that?"

"No," he said dryly. "It was not. But it's gone now. What were you saying before?"

"Nothing really. Just that Julia looked happy, and that she and Charles were probably very much in love."

A sudden stirring in the air startled her into looking up. It was as though a cool wind had suddenly started blowing upon her. "Gabe?" she whispered. "Do you feel . . ."

"Rose water."

The open folder sailed off the wicker trunk. Angie stared in disbelief. She had the eerie feeling that an unseen hand had just swept angrily over the glass top, scattering papers everywhere.

"Holy cow." She covered her wildly beating heart with her hand.

"Rose water," she heard Gabriel murmur again.

As the last paper fluttered down to the floor, Angie

slowly turned her head to stare at him. "What was that all about?"

"I think," he said quietly, "Julia is trying to tell us that hers was not a marriage made in heaven."

Somehow that wasn't the answer she'd expected. Then again, she wasn't certain what explanation she'd expected him to magically produce. "How do you know that?"

"I just know."

She kept silent for a moment, knowing that arguing against his intuition, or clairvoyance, or whatever the heck it was, was futile. He'd turned out to be right too many times.

"I know, too," he said, "that we have a hundred-year-old mystery to solve."

"*We?*" She stared at him, feeling she'd just entered the Twilight Zone.

"You and me, pretty lady. We're definitely in this thing together." He put an arm around her and gently pulled her head onto his shoulder.

"How are *we* supposed to solve this mystery?"

He shrugged. "I don't know everything. I guess we follow wherever Julia leads."

Lies!

Julia fled up the staircase, sobs choking her throat.

She ran from the mockery of her lying face in the photograph and the memory of the cruel way Charles had dug his punishing fingers into her side as a reminder that he expected her to show the world a bride's happy smile.

She ran from the naïveté of youth, which had not allowed her to see the evil in Charles, which had not allowed her to imagine that the fine new house he built for his bride would not be her home, but her eternal prison.

Lies. Wicked, wicked lies!

Nothing would induce Angie to stay in the bedroom where the light bulbs had exploded, so that night she moved into another one. In one of the two quaint twin beds, she lay awake, staring at the ceiling, thinking of Gabriel, and wondering if he was awake and thinking of her. He was in the next room, just a short walk away— or one loud scream away, if anything strange should happen.

An aching aloneness flowed through her. Loneliness was something she didn't think about often. She had Miles, her family, and good friends. But as though Gabriel had been a part of her life for years instead of days, she missed him, was lonely for him.

She flipped over on her side and reached out to the bedside table to turn on the clock radio. A little music would fill up the lonely silence and chase her blues away.

A lively song came on. Angie lay back and listened. She wasn't a big country and western fan, but the tune was cheerful and the words were catchy.

Suddenly the music ceased. She elbowed upright and tapped the side of the radio. Nothing happened. She fiddled with the "on" and "off" buttons. Nothing. For the heck of it, she played with the tuner, and the radio came on again.

Scanning the stations, she found a rock 'n' roll one she liked. Her head had barely touched the pillow when Bruce Springsteen's voice faded away and the radio went silent again.

It was probably shorting out, she thought. Making a mental note to purchase a new clock radio for this guest room, she rolled over and grabbed the cord, intending to unplug it. Before she could give it a yank, though, music wafted from the small speakers.

A fraction of a second was all it took for her to realize that what she was hearing wasn't Springsteen but a recording of "Waltz of the Flowers" from Tchaikovsky's *Nutcracker Suite*.

A chill crept up Angie's spine. The station had been changed. She hit the "off" button. The music ceased for a heartbeat, then came on again.

She instinctively drew the covers up to her chin. She peered around the room, looking for shadows, looking for a Tchaikovsky-loving ghost. "Go away," she whispered.

The music stopped, and in the silence that followed Angie could have sworn she heard a soft, regretful sigh.

Don't be a nervous Nelly, she told herself. There was no sighing, Tchaikovsky-loving ghost in the room. No monsters under the bed or in the closet. She was probably asleep, dreaming she was awake and . . .

Like heck she was!

Sitting bolt upright, Angie threw the covers off. She pulled a robe on over her nightgown and made a mad dash out into the hall.

Quickly covering the short distance to Gabriel's room, she entered without knocking. The drapes hadn't been drawn over the windows and twilight filtered in, casting a pale gloom over the bed.

Staring at Gabriel, she forgot for a moment why she was there. He lay on his side, hugging a pillow. He was naked to the waist as far as she could tell. Naked, beautiful, and sound asleep.

Have mercy! She fought the shaky feeling invading her limbs and the sweet longing filling her breasts. Heady memories of that night came tumbling back. Passionate kisses and whimsical moments. A romantic candlelight dinner. Going out to look at the moon and count the stars. Lying on the sofa in the den for hours, caressing each other through their clothes, whispering and laughing and trading more passionate kisses.

As she feasted on the sight of him, she told herself she could be in his arms right now. Her body was ready. Her emotions were engaged. Her mind was . . .

Just not ready to make that quantum leap.

"Gabe," she whispered urgently, leaning down to touch his forearm.

"Uh?" he grunted, rearing his head up. "Angie?" He let go of the pillow he was hugging and tossed it aside. Sitting up, he turned on the lamp and blinked up at her like a sleepy owl.

"Something's happened. I need you."

He gave her a groggy smile. "I need you too. Have you come to fulfill all my fantasies?"

On some levels Angie was very secure. His words, though, touched a deep and hidden pocket of insecurity, and she felt a measure of hurt. A fantasy. Was that what she was to him? A ninth-grade boy's fantasy girl?

She tucked that small wound into the back of her mind and responded lightly, "This is no time to joke around."

"Who's joking?"

She groaned. "Please, Gabe. We have to talk."

"Oh, all right. Just a minute." Gabriel grabbed his glasses off the nightstand, shoved them on, and the blur that was Angie came sharply and oh so erotically into focus.

She was wearing a silky jade robe that barely covered her thighs. Underneath was a short little nothing of a nightgown that dipped over her perfect breasts. The feminine garments were made for seduction. Unfortunately, the woman in them hadn't come to seduce.

"I wondered if you wore contacts," she said, breaking into his regretful thoughts.

He hoped she wasn't suddenly seeing him as the geeky kid who'd worn ugly glasses with lenses thick as the bottoms of old Coke bottles. "Most of the time I do wear contacts. Do you hate the glasses?"

"I like them," she responded with a decisive nod. "Makes you look like the genius you are." She smiled impishly. "There's no truth in the old saying that women don't make passes at men who wear glasses."

He laughed as he drew her down to sit with him. "I thought it was, boys don't make passes at girls who wear glasses."

"Boys and girls are fickle creatures. Adults have more sense."

"You're so beautiful," he murmured. His fingers wandered with delicacy over her face—her brows, her eyelids, her nose and lips.

His touch, as always, made Angie's heart beat faster. "Is this a pass?"

He held on to her hand. "It's whatever you want it to be. I'm content just to be with you."

Handsome and not knowing it, incredibly clever without conceit, sweet and sincere, he was more than she could resist, and she did the thing she had promised herself she wouldn't do again that night: She bent forward and kissed his irresistible mouth. She heard him take a slight breath that might have been surprise or pleasure, then felt his mouth become a willing captive.

His hands shifted on her, drawing her onto his lap. He twisted, lowering her to the bed, which felt warm from contact with his body, and he followed her down, covering her mouth in a long, sublime kiss.

Angie felt his body harden, his manhood press against her thigh. Her fingers trailed down the length of his arm to his hip. She shuddered. He was completely nude!

She stirred and turned her head to one side as she

waged a fierce battle against total surrender. "I'm sorry. I didn't mean to start something I can't finish tonight."

"Don't be sorry." Gabriel was light-headed from wanting her, and he struggled to subdue the need flaming in him.

He sensed need in her, too, but he also sensed a hesitancy to give her emotions free rein. He was frustrated that he didn't understand the source of it. Was it caused by something he had said or done? Or something he hadn't said or done?

He sat with his back against the mahogany sleigh bed, pulled the bed linens up to his waist, then drew her up beside him. "You said something happened."

"The ghost was in my room."

He curled his arm around her shoulders, pulling her closer. "How do you know Julia was in your room? What did she do? Are you all right? Were you scared?" His questions tumbled out one after the other, accompanied by a flare of concern in his eyes.

Angie couldn't stop herself from melting against him. "She was playing with the radio. I wasn't frightened. It sure made me nervous, though. And by the way, it gives me the willies to hear you call the ghost Julia. Makes her sound like a real person."

"She is. Or was at one time." He laughed softly at the face she made, and hugged her. "Tell me what happened with the radio."

She told him about how the radio had gone on and off, how she'd thought the wiring was going bad, how the station had changed from rock to classical without her having touched the dial, finishing with how it had come back on even after she'd turned it off. When she finished, Gabriel was quiet for a long moment.

"So?" she asked him finally. "What do you think?"

"I ought to be exercising a little critical doubt. If we searched hard enough, we might find a normal, acceptable explanation. But I have a feeling you're right in thinking Julia did it."

"I was hoping you'd try to talk me out of thinking that," she said heavily. "I even thought I heard—" She stopped speaking and shook her head.

"What did you hear?" he prompted.

"I thought I heard someone sigh, and it wasn't me." She laughed at herself. "Probably my imagination. At that point I was ready to see monsters under the bed."

"Maybe. Maybe not." He looked down into her face. "Are you up for an experiment? I'd like to repeat the sequence of events and see what manifests."

She started to object, but didn't. Curiosity shone eagerly in his eyes. "Oh, all right."

He beamed a smile at her. "That's my girl."

So much was in his face: desire, approval, that eagerness to explore the unknown, and a kind of gentle amusement.

"Am I?" she heard herself say on a shaky breath.

"Are you mine? Is that what you're asking?" His thumb smoothed along her jaw, moving back and forth, his gaze searching.

Unable to trust herself to speak, she nodded.

Very softly, he said, "I can want what I want from now until eternity, pretty lady." His hand came to rest under her chin and lifted her face. He spoke even softer. "But only you can answer that question. What's happening inside your mind? Your heart?"

She tried to put her thoughts into words. "The world as I know it has turned upside down. I'm experiencing firsthand things I didn't believe in a few days ago. I can't go back to the familiar patterns, even if I wanted to." She started to turn her face away, but his hand brought her back. "I—I have feelings for you. But surely you know that. You seem to be able to read me like a book."

"Sometimes," he answered solemnly. "But most of the time, my feelings for you seem to block out my ability to read yours."

"Then you do feel something for me?"

"Oh yes, I most certainly do."

Never had she been more fascinated by his eyes, by the mystery of their color, the light-reflecting gray that warmed rather than cooled. "What do you want? What do you hope will happen between us?"

His expression changed, becoming tender. "A few days ago I stood outside this house, knowing something good waited for me inside. That something good is you. I want to be yours and I want you to be mine."

She felt a smile start deep inside her, as much sensation as emotion. It flowered and grew until it spread across her face.

He smiled in return, then seemed to pull back slightly, as though careful not to let their emotions get the better of them.

"Are you ready to tackle that experiment with the radio in your room?" he asked.

She nodded. She was a mere heartbeat away from agreeing to tackle any experiment he wanted to try, a heartbeat away from vowing to follow him to the ends of the earth and beyond.

"Then close your eyes, love. I've got to put on my pants."

Laughing, she complied.

An hour later, Gabriel lay half-awake in one of the twin beds in Angie's room. Any critical doubt that remained in him had been banished when his experiment with the radio had produced the same interesting results Angie had experienced. Afterward, she hadn't wanted to be alone, and he had offered to stay.

As he listened to the even sound of her breathing coming from the other bed, a flood of emotions washed through him: a restful sense of contentment; a fierce desire to protect the woman he loved; a frightening realization of how important she was to him.

Even before he'd walked into the mansion that first day, he'd sensed it was his destiny to be there. When he'd walked into the kitchen, he had been rocked by Angie's beauty and by a feeling that they were meant to be together; that one way or another they would have found each other, even if Ivy Rule hadn't acted to bring them together when she did. Their relationship seemed inevitable, and so right.

Destiny. It was a concept he had never given much thought to. If anyone had asked him a week ago if he believed in destiny, he would probably have said the same thing he would have said about ghosts, that he didn't believe in it but he had an open mind on the subject. Now it seemed natural, an undeniable truth, that everyone had a destiny to fulfill and that his lay with this lovely woman.

Smiling, Gabriel drifted into a restful sleep.

In the other bed, Angie sighed as the dream came upon her. She was aware of the strength and warmth of his flesh as she walked hand in hand with him along the fieldstone path that led to Julia's garden. Being with him made her feel so good, she didn't pause to wonder where the scent of roses was coming from. She breathed in the sweet fragrance, feeling glad to be alive, glad just to be with him.

Being in love again gave her such joy that she wanted to laugh out loud. She wanted to dance, not walk solemnly, toward their destination. . . .

ELEVEN

Late the next evening Angie decided to follow her heart. Now, as she wandered around Gabriel's room, she felt as excited and as nervous as a virgin bride on her wedding night.

She picked up a white dress shirt he'd left draped over the back of a chair and pressed it to her nose. No obvious scent clung to the fabric. Apparently, Gabriel favored the use of soap, water, and the very lightest of after-shaves.

Liking the notion of wearing something that had touched his skin, she put her arms through the sleeves and drew the shirt around her. For a moment she stood holding the ends of the collar close to her throat.

Then she went over to the bed and pulled back the covers. Sitting on the edge of the mattress with her hands folded made her feel like a silly schoolgirl. She swung her legs up and tried arranging herself in a not-too-obvious but seductive pose. That felt even sillier. So she sat up and wrapped her arms around her bent legs.

"Angie baby," she said in amused self-disgust. "It's been too long."

She considered herself an accomplished flirt. But flirting was just about all she'd ever done with any man besides Jon. She laughed softly as she thought how shocked most of her acquaintances would be if they knew she wasn't the merry widow they perceived her to be.

Gabriel didn't know she was waiting for him. He thought she'd retired to the lonely twin bed in the next room.

She laughed a little as she imagined him downstairs, fussing with his electronic toys. He'd taken to playing little games, moving his expensive gadgets from one place to another, then hiding to see if he could catch his ghost in the act of putting it all out of commission. She found it highly entertaining that Julia always outwitted him.

"Hurry, Gabriel," she whispered. She could hardly sit still knowing what she had planned for him that night.

If Gabriel wasn't pleasantly surprised to find her there, she knew her face would turn a brighter shade of red than the skimpy bodysuit she wore. If he didn't desire her as much as she desired him, she didn't think she'd be able to bear it.

Gabriel paused halfway up the staircase and leaned over the banister to look at the still camera on its tripod and the light stands he'd set up and double-checked in the foyer. The lace doily draped over the camera lens had not been there a few minutes ago.

"Give a poor parapsychologist a break, Julia," he pleaded, glancing around just in case she was near and listening. "One picture. That's all I need. Please." He looked hopefully down below. The doily remained in place.

Returning to the foyer to uncover the lens would be a waste of time. He knew she'd simply throw the piece of lace over the camera the minute his back was turned.

He sighed and continued on to his room, his thoughts turning to more satisfying and pleasant things.

The bright, warm Sunday had called him and Angie out to play. They'd taken Miles to lunch and to a Disney movie. As they'd left the theater, a woman had smiled at him and said, "It's so nice to see a family doing things together." For the rest of the day, those words had remained a warm spot in his mind.

He'd been a little apprehensive about having dinner with Angie's friends, Nila and Jake Madison. It had turned out all right, though, and he'd enjoyed their company.

Just before leaving the Madisons' at nine, he'd helped Angie tuck her son into bed. Miles had shyly given him a good-night hug, which had been a new experience for Gabriel. The moment had been so disarming and satisfying, he had found himself longing to hear the boy say, "Good night, Daddy," instead of "Good night, Dr. Richards."

Most of all, though, he'd treasured the time spent with Angie. She was a perfect companion: bright, vital, fun, generous, erotically sexy and passionate. He loved looking at her, touching her, talking with her. Even their silences were comfortable, neither feeling that awkward need to fill every minute with conversation.

Beautiful, loving, giving Angie. He wanted her in every way a man could want a woman: as a friend, lover, wife, partner, mother of his children. . . .

By the time Gabriel entered his room, his mind was so thoroughly preoccupied with Angie, he first thought he had simply conjured up her image. It took him a second to make the adjustment from imagination to reality.

She really was there, sitting in the middle of his bed, arms wrapped around her knees. She was wearing only a smile and a little scrap of red cloth beneath his shirt.

"Do you know why I'm here?" she asked, looking up at him with dreamy blue eyes.

"I have several optimistic fantasies on the subject." He felt light-headed as he closed the door behind him. "I want to do the right thing, so perhaps it would be best if you *told* me why you're here."

Seeing the passion that sprang to life in his eyes and knowing he was concerned about doing the right thing, Angie fell even more deeply in love with him. "I can't wait anymore, Gabe. I need you."

His rapturous smile warmed her. "That was one of my fantasies."

"Do you need me?" she asked softly as she shifted to tuck her legs beneath her.

"More than you'll ever know."

Gabriel watched a smile sweep over her beautiful mouth. She slipped her hands beneath her hair and lifted the golden mass high, then let it slowly fall. It was one of the most erotically feminine gestures he had ever seen. Hypnotic as a flame, she lifted her hair again, letting it drift down around her like a caress.

"Love at first sight," she murmured. "*Coup de foudre*, the French call it." She got to her knees, her gaze never wavering from his. She smiled. "Do you believe in love at first sight, Gabe?"

"I didn't until I met you again. Now I do. I love you, pretty lady."

"I love you back." Her smile grew into something mischievous and sexy. With a smooth undulation of her shoulders, she sent his shirt slithering to her waist.

His heated gaze traveled over the thin red cotton molded to her body. The bodysuit was low-cut, cupping and making the delicious most of her small breasts.

She raised her arms, stretching out her hands to him. "Please," was all she said in a voice so soft, so intense, it robbed him of breath and made his heart hammer against his chest. Her wildness was a siren's song, drawing him to her.

Gabriel kicked off his shoes, stripped away his socks, then joined her on the bed. He knelt with her and she wrapped his waist in her arms. For a long moment they remained close, holding each other, savoring the joy that they would be together as only a man and woman could be.

"I want to feel what it is to be a part of you," she said, looking solemnly into his eyes.

"I want that too." He stroked her upper arms, his palms moving in slow, shaky circles.

Their mouths met, creating wonder and excitement. Their hands became playful emissaries that searched and teased and thrilled.

Breaking away to laugh for the simple pleasure of it, Gabriel spread his hands over her rib cage. He swept them upward to cover her breasts, lifting them and lightly squeezing as he bent to kiss the valley between them. With the tip of his tongue he traced the edge of her bodice, tasting the texture of the fabric, breathing in the enticing scent of her perfume.

He looked up. "You have a dreamer's eyes. What do they dream about, Angie?"

"You. They dream about you." She opened his shirt, discovering again the feel of his naked chest. How wonderfully made he was of hard muscle and soft, warm skin.

Angie thought to inquire about his dreams, but his lips touched hers and the thought was lost. She kissed him as she'd never kissed before, too joy-filled to be concerned with technique, too much in love to care. He accepted the silly kisses, the light strokes, the deeper ones, and returned the love play with a joy of his own.

When respiration became rapid sighs and cheeks became flushed, they drew back to look at each other with brilliant, love-dazed eyes. Gently, he stripped away her bodysuit and tossed it to the floor. In between their touching and exploring, she helped him remove the rest of his clothing.

Gabriel lifted her, laying her down on her back. His mouth dipped to kiss her navel, then the erect tips of her breasts. He loved the way she plunged her fingers into his hair, murmuring his name over and over as he teased and tasted and brushed the undersides of breasts, stomach, and thighs.

She trembled, feeling alive, feeling fire and ice in all the places he touched. Her mouth found his again with urgent heat as she received his knee between her thighs and reveled in its exquisite movement against her feminine core. He slipped a hand beneath her and palmed her bottom, rocking his body against hers until they both became frantic for their joining.

Gabriel took a breath to steady himself. He raised up to gaze down into her face, loving the deep passion transforming her eyes into glowing blue stars.

"Angie," he said, when he could find his voice. "I wasn't—I'm not prepared for this. We can stop now and just hold each other, if you want."

She lifted her hand and stroked his cheek. "Yesterday I took the liberty of purchasing what we need. I hope you don't mind. It's there on the table."

He showed her he didn't mind with a kiss that stole her breath and made her laugh. He left her long enough to prepare himself. Then they started all over again, learning how and where the other liked to be touched.

Love whispered through Gabriel, and in the delirium of passion he spoke to her in guileless words, half-sentences, erotic phrases. His mouth curved into a hazy smile as he looked into her eyes, while slowly, by exquisite measures, he euphorically sank himself into her body.

Pleasure shuddered through Angie. She had prayed for someone to love. Those prayers had been answered. God had sent her a miracle in the form of this man.

They moved together in rhythm, sharing the grandeur of a single vision more eloquent than any language could express.

Angie sighed as the sweet dream came upon her. She breathed in the scent of rose permeating the air as she walked with Gabriel along the fieldstone path. . . .

Gabriel stirred without waking. Instinctively, he reached out and hugged Angie to him as he shared her dream of strolling through Julia's garden.

❦ ———————— ❦

Angie spent the better part of Monday in the newspaper's morgue, seeking out every piece of information she could find about Julia Rose Kingston.

Early that evening she sat with Gabriel in a wicker loveseat on the side porch, relating her findings while they watched the day end in a blaze of glory.

"Julia Rose was a much-sought-after young lady before she married Kingston," Angie told him. "She was a diamond of the first water, as they used to say."

Gabriel managed to look suitably interested, though it surprised him to find that his greater interest at the moment was playing with Angie's hair. "What else did you learn about her?" He wound a golden strand tightly around one finger, making the tip of his finger turn white.

"My great-grandfather, Miles Luke, was one of Julia's suitors."

"Really?" That piece of information piqued his curiosity and won his full attention. "That would be Ivy's and Clover's grandfather?"

She nodded. "I found at least a dozen references in the society pages of him having escorted her to various parties, outings, and a debutante ball. Apparently, though, she dropped him like a hot potato after Kingston came into the picture, and he became her sole escort."

"I wonder," he murmured, releasing the silky blonde strand.

"Wonder what?"

"Your Miles said that the Shadow Lady sometimes came to his room here at the inn, and that she sat in a chair beside his bed as though she was watching over him. I wonder if Julia was doing just that—keeping an old lover's namesake safe from harm."

She gave him a startled look. "Do you think it's possible she feels some kind of connection with my family because of her relationship with my great-grandfather?"

"It's possible."

"Spooky." She was silent for a second. "I just had a bizarre thought. What if Julia married Kingston for his money, but she continued to see Miles Luke on the sly . . . in the garden I—I mean we—dreamed about." It had blown her mind to discover that Gabriel had had the same dream the night before, down to the smallest detail.

"It's possible, I suppose. I think the most logical explanation is that she's trying to tell us something."

"Like what?"

He shrugged. "I don't know yet." He didn't understand the significance of why Julia kept leading them to her garden in the dream. But love was broadening his faith in all things, and he believed that Julia would help him understand when the time was right. "What else did you learn from your research?"

"After she became engaged to Kingston, the society pages were full of the usual rounds of engagement parties, bridal teas, and such. Their wedding was reported on in lavish detail. When they came back from a month's honeymoon in Europe, the references to their participation in various events ceased after a few months. Charles was mentioned a few times for making large contributions to various charities, but it seems as though Julia withdrew completely from society."

He exchanged a glance with her. "Maybe Charles was the jealous type and he wanted to keep his young bride to himself."

"Maybe. She didn't make the news until her death two years after her marriage." Angie paused, knowing Gabriel wasn't going to like what she had to report next. "According to the newspaper account, Julia had suffered from some undisclosed illness since the beginning of her marriage. Kingston finally sent her away for treatment. Gabe, she died somewhere in Europe."

"No," he said softly but firmly. "That's simply not possible. Julia died in this house."

"But the newspaper article said—"

"I don't care what it said. She didn't die somewhere else. I don't know how I know that, but I do."

They were silent, contemplating the conflicting information. The setting sun was a hazy palette of color on the horizon. The balmy breeze moving through the trees was like a chorus of murmuring voices.

"All right," Angie finally said, turning her head to look up into his pensive face. "If you believe she died here, then I believe it too."

He smiled at her. "Thank you for believing in me. Have I told you that I love everything about you?"

The muscles in Angie's stomach fluttered amid the heat of desire that exploded deep inside her. "You just love my cooking . . . and other things," she teased.

He grinned. "I do love your cooking . . . and I especially love your other things." His gaze lowered to her breasts. "I also love your face, your voice." He pulled her onto his lap, and his tongue and lips tantalized the corner of her mouth before stealing her breath in hungry possession.

The friction of his hard chest against her breasts and the intoxicating strength of his kisses caused tremors of pleasure to wash over Angie. Her teasing tongue slipped into the moist depths of his mouth, her body melted against his. She could feel the instant heat of his manhood pressing against her hip. They might as well have been naked.

He pulled his mouth from her kiss-swollen lips to burrow his face in her cloud of golden hair. "Do you know how many times I wanted to kiss you like that in high school?" he said, his voice thick and husky. He raised his hand to caress one of her breasts through her blouse. The nipple responded instantly, swelling into his palm. "I loved everything about you then. The way you looked, the way you walked and talked . . ."

Then? Angie smiled—but she felt a bit uneasy, just the same.

"That silver-bell laugh of yours drove me crazy in geometry class." He nuzzled her forehead with his nose. "You're every fantasy I've ever had, come true."

She winced at the word "fantasy." Her heart erupted in a frantic rhythm; her limbs went rigid. She felt as though her body temperature dropped to the freezing point.

He sensed the change and looked at her. "What's wrong?"

"I'm not a fantasy." Her hands pushed against his chest as she tried to twist away, but he easily captured her wrists.

"You are to me." His eyes were passion-filled, half-hooded. "You've been my fantasy since the first time I saw you in Mrs. Adams's geometry class."

She stared at him, her own eyes wide and wounded. "I don't want to be anyone's fantasy."

"You're upset," he said, frowning. "I thought it would please you to know you've always been my dream girl."

"I want to be your reality, not some leftover childhood fantasy of yours."

He laughed, then cradled her face between his hands. "You are my reality, pretty lady. I love you. You've captured my mind, my heart, my very soul."

Angie allowed him to kiss her. She even kissed him back, with passion. Still, uneasy thoughts lingered in her mind. What if his feelings for her were unconsciously based on the high school freshman girl he'd known rather than the woman she was today? It would break her heart into a million pieces, that's what if.

"Gabe," she whispered shakily as she drew back to look at him. "I fear we've rushed into this relationship."

He regarded her steadily for several seconds before he asked quietly, "Do you regret making love with me?"

"No." She slid off his lap and walked to the edge of the porch. Bracing one hand on a supporting column, she gazed out to the delicate shadows the sunset had spread over the rhododendrons and magnolias.

"Are you saying you aren't sure you love me?"

"No, that's not what I mean."

"I don't understand, Angie. I thought everything was going so well between us."

"Everything *is* going well. It's just that on many levels we're still intimate strangers."

"Yes, but not for long. That's what a courtship is all about—getting to know each other." She heard him sigh heavily before he asked, "Is there something you think I'm not saying or doing? If there is, please tell me."

"There isn't anything you haven't said or done right." That was only half-true. She wished he would swear he loved her for who she was now, and that he would love her forever.

Her wishes struck her as foolishly girlish. A soft laugh of self-rebuke escaped her.

"Want to share the joke?" His tone was one of bewildered hurt.

"I was just laughing at myself," she responded, turning to lean against the column.

He watched her with troubled eyes. "Your emotions are bouncing around like Mexican jumping beans. I sense I've disappointed you or hurt you in some way."

"You haven't really. It's just old insecurities trying to get their claws in me."

Gabriel sensed uncertainty trembling like a small animal in her mind. Was she feeling more vulnerable, more open to pain and rejection, now that they had crossed a line in their relationship by becoming lovers?

What about the way she'd reacted to being called his fantasy, his dream girl? Did it have something to do with a fear of being loved only for superficial things and not for herself? Everyone got crucified in some way or the other during their youth, he thought. He sensed that now in her, and he understood why the idea of being his fantasy disturbed her.

Angie watched him get up and walk toward her. He spoke her name as if it were a sweet melody, and she suddenly felt too full inside, as though something foreign and unwanted was swelling and struggling to get out through her skin.

"I readily admit I want to possess your body." His smile was slow and sensual. "But it's not because I had a crush on you light-years ago. It's because you're the most sensuous *woman* I've ever met."

He made no move to touch her with anything but his words. "I'm no young boy. I know what I feel and I know what I want. I don't want Angie Sinclair, the freshman class beauty. I want Angie Sinclair Parker, the woman whose strength of mind and heart I have come to admire tremendously, the woman who has a boundless capacity for giving unselfishly to everyone around her."

His voice reached out to soothe her. "You are of value for all those qualities and more—like your intelligence and your spirit."

She stared into his eyes as emotion and need swept through her. She still felt too full inside, only now it was a good feeling. "Thank you, my love. I needed to hear that."

Reaching up, he put one fingertip on her temple and slowly traced her hairline. "Before I met you, I didn't know I could love so deeply."

Heat followed his finger and found its way through the rest of her. She moved to press herself against him, wanting to feel his hands on her. "How deeply?"

"It has no measure." He lowered his mouth to kiss her lightly once, twice. The third kiss was hungry, impatient, and achingly sweet.

"Time is slipping by so fast," Angie said to Gabriel several days later. They were walking toward the north edge of the property, to the garden that had played a part in both their dreams since they'd become lovers. "Sometimes I wish I could capture time, lock it up in a magic box, and whenever I opened the box out would fly all the precious memories and thoughts contained in that time."

"If I could, I would conjure up that magic box for you." He smiled and squeezed her hand, making her aware of the strength and warmth of his flesh.

Her love for Gabriel was growing stronger, and she no longer feared she was nothing more to him than a boy's fantasy.

She couldn't stop touching him, kissing him, running her hands over him. They engaged in endless hours of lovemaking, during which they both flew to the limits of ecstasy. And they spent hours talking about silly things, serious things—everything but what would happen to them when it came time for him to leave.

Time. There was that word again, she thought with a second's dismay.

Pressing close to his side, Angie refused to concentrate on anything more than the clear joy of this moment. Being with him made her feel so good. So alive. She wanted to laugh out loud for no reason. She wanted to dance, not walk solemnly, toward their destination.

As they neared the area they'd come to see, she was almost disappointed to find that it didn't look anything like it had in the dream. It wasn't a garden at all, just a small section of land that had been allowed to grow wild.

The sun filtered sporadically through the thick copse of trees, throwing patches of light over the jungle of tangled vines and flowering shrubs. Weeds grew with abandon between uneven fieldstones sunk into the ground.

There was nothing here, she thought. Nothing but an eerie stillness.

"I used to play here. Did I tell you that?" Gabriel said as they came to the tumbled-down gazebo.

"No, you didn't."

He released her hand and started circling the pile of rotted and broken wood. "I didn't have any close friends, so I spent a lot of time alone."

A faint smile played upon his lips as he glanced at her. "Sometimes I pretended you were Sleeping Beauty, and the evil witch had locked you up inside the mansion, doomed to sleep through eternity unless I could rescue you with a kiss."

Laughter bubbled up inside her. "A hopeless romantic, that's you, Gabriel Richards."

"Not hope*less*—hope*ful*. I love you, Angie."

Love and desire hit her like the hard backwash of a wave. "Then come kiss me, rescue me from the witch's evil spell."

Gabriel had taken only a single step toward her when he froze. The air around him had grown so heavy with the scent of roses he couldn't breathe. A terrible sadness struck him so hard, he swayed on his feet.

"Gabe?"

He looked up at the sound of Angie's faraway voice. Her face was blurry. Everything around him blurred as emotions and images rushed through his mind so rapidly, they were no more than a collage of nebulous impressions. But one presence was paramount throughout it all. Julia. The sound of her weeping filled his ears, his mind, his heart.

He stumbled backward, tripping, falling hard. The earth where he lay sprawled seemed alive with one powerful human emotion: *blind hatred*.

Bolting upright, he held up his hands to ward off the blurry figure coming at him. "No!"

"It's all right. It's just me. I love you." Angie's sweet voice, and the love he heard in the words she kept saying over and over, slowly pulled him out of the darkness and back into the light.

TWELVE

The solid masculine body under the blanket didn't move when Angie quietly let herself into the room. She figured Gabriel was still sleeping off the experience he'd had in the jungle that she could no longer bring herself to call a garden. He'd fallen into a deep, exhausted sleep soon after she'd brought him back to the house, and he'd been out cold for six hours.

She undressed and eased into bed beside him.

"Sleeping Beauty to the fallen warrior's rescue."

Hearing his voice gave her a momentary start, and she jerked. She turned her head and saw that his eyes were open, watching her.

"You're awake," she answered softly. "How do you feel?"

"Better." He reached out and drew her close, slipping his arms around her waist.

She rubbed the side of her face against his chest,

pleased with his warmth, with the strong and steady beat of his heart. His hands locked together behind her back, giving her a feeling of being encircled by his sweet strength.

"I scared you out there, didn't I?"

She raised her head. Her eyes had adjusted to the dark, and she could see his wonderful face. "It was awful, knowing something was wrong, knowing I couldn't share whatever you were seeing and feeling." She shuddered, recalling everything he'd told her about what had happened to him there. "I thank God and all the guardian angels in heaven that I wasn't born with your psychic gift. I don't know how you stand it."

His soft laughter feathered like a kiss over her face. "It's like anything else you're born with or acquire somewhere along the way: You get used to it, learn to live with it, and you adjust."

"Gabe, I—"

"Hush, pretty lady." His mouth sealed hers with a kiss. He rolled her over, and she snaked her arms around his neck.

Slowly, enticingly, he moved against her, kissing her with an almost desperate fervor. Soon she was moving with him through space and time, moving through all the vivid colors and sensations her mind could imagine and her body could feel.

Her orgasm hit her like a burst of sunlight, radiating out from the deep center of her. She tightened her legs around his hips and moaned his name as each blinding ray of ecstasy traveled through her body. Then she felt his shattering release pulsating inside her.

Neither of them moved for a long time, not wanting to break the bond between them.

"I love you," Gabriel said, kissing her damp temple. He eased onto his side, but kept her cradled against him.

"I think I know what Julia wants."

"Mmmm," he said, not in response to her statement, but in reaction to the feel of her fingers skimming his forearm. "What does she want?"

"To be buried beside my great-grandfather." She spoke so softly that for a second he thought he must have heard her wrong.

She drew away from him a little and raised up on her elbow. "I found something while you were sleeping." She hesitated for a moment. "Actually, I didn't find it. Julia did everything but lead me by the nose to the place where she hid her journal."

"A journal?" Gabriel let out a whistle. "No kidding? Where was it?"

"In the room where she did her exploding light bulb trick. It was in a little cubbyhole behind a couple of bricks in the fireplace."

She told him how the lights inside that room had come on as she had been on her way downstairs, after he had fallen asleep. "I was so ticked off at her for what she'd put you through in her damned garden that I went in to tell her she was a rude, annoying ghost."

He laughed.

"Glad you think it's amusing," she said dryly. "You could have been hurt out there."

"But I wasn't. Go on. I can't wait to hear how you faced off with poor old Julia."

"Well, I never quite got around to it. As I was looking for a shadow to yell at, I saw—stop grinning at me!—I saw that two bricks were missing from the left side of the fireplace. Like an idiot, I stuck my hand in the cubbyhole and came out with a leather-bound book about the size of a large index card and about a half-inch thick. The binding was worn and cracked in a few places, and the pages had yellowed, but it was okay otherwise.

"I opened it to the first page, and let me tell you, the first sentence shocked the hell out of me. Julia had written: *Charles is insane.*"

"No sh—sugar," Gabriel said, calling back the swear-word and substituting her euphemism.

"Kingston was one sick puppy." She shivered, and he put both arms around her in an unconscious protective gesture. "Julia didn't want to marry him. She was in love with my great-grandfather. But Kingston was wealthier. So I guess that made him a better catch than Miles Luke, and her family pressured her into marrying him. She didn't like him much, but she didn't know what a creep he really was until he started flying into jealous rages on their honeymoon and began browbeating her every time he imagined she'd even looked at another man.

"After they moved into this house, he slowly cut her off from society, and even from her own family. He told everyone that the state of her health and mind was too delicate to sustain the rigors of company."

Angie stirred restlessly, and Gabriel turned to draw her head onto his shoulder. She put her arm around his neck and buried her face in the hollow of his throat. "The garden surrounding the gazebo was the only place he let her go. It was her escape. Eventually, he stopped allowing her even that."

"Then what happened?" he asked, nestling his face to the side of hers.

"That was about it. Except for the last entry." Her sigh rippled over his skin. "It was . . . it moved me. Really moved me, Gabe."

"What did it say?"

"She said she longed to see her beloved Miles's face, but feared she would not see him again until they both stood at the gates of heaven. That's how I know that Julia wants to be buried beside him. But how we'll ever find her to do that, I don't know."

"I think I know."

"Okay, Mr. Psychic." She winnowed her fingers through his hair. "Where is she?"

"Near the gazebo. I think I fell on her."

"Holy cow." She stared at him for a moment, then asked, "What do you think happened to her?"

He shrugged. "I don't know. I doubt we'll ever know what really happened."

"We're lucky," Angie whispered after awhile. "We have each other here and now."

They held each other all through the night, making love and reveling in the warmth of that greatest of all human joys.

Two days later, they stood at the edge of the northernmost tip of the property. The morning had dawned fair and hot in Danville. A crew of workmen were clearing away a hundred years of neglect, and several other men were digging in the place near the ruined gazebo that Gabriel had pointed out to them.

Suddenly there was a shout of discovery, and the men who were digging threw down their shovels, dropped to their knees, and began working the earth with their hands.

Angie's heart was in her throat as she looked at Gabriel. "It's over, isn't it?"

"Yes, I think it's over."

She turned away and started for the house.

"Wait." He caught her from behind, wrapping his arms around her. "It's over for Julia, but not for us."

She stared straight ahead. "I'm afraid it probably is.— I want to marry you, Gabe, or end it right here and now."

"Are you serious?"

"Yes. I've been thinking about it a lot." She placed her hands over his.

"So have I. And *I* want to marry *you*."

She was stunned. "Do you love—honestly, truly, deeply love me?"

He rubbed his cheek against her silky hair.

"With all my heart."

She let out a sigh that seemed to come from the depths of her soul. "We're a package deal, Miles and me. A child—your own or someone else's—is a lifetime responsibility. Are you ready for that?"

"It would be my pleasure, my joy, to share the responsibility of raising Miles."

"I want more children."

Gabriel turned her, swept her up into his arms, and swung around in a circle. "Let's start now. When you do want to get married? Today? Tomorrow? Don't make me wait. Where do you want to get married? Do you want to live here or with me in Durham?"

She laughed at his rapid-fire questions, and held on tight to him.

Gabriel lowered her to her feet. The sun filtering through the trees cast ribbons of light and shadow over her beautiful face, and he touched his mouth to hers to drink the pure Virginia sunshine from her lips.

Tipping her head back to look at him, she smiled, and he was mesmerized by the joy she created in him. "I want to marry you as soon as possible," she said as she caressed his cheek with the back of her hand. "Julia had to wait an eternity to be with her beloved. I don't want to wait a minute longer than necessary to be with mine forever."

EPILOGUE

A year had passed since Julia's remains had been discovered buried in the back garden and then been lain to rest beside Angie's great-grandfather, Miles Luke.

Ivy had recovered from her accident, and had returned to doing what she loved best: spoiling her guests at the Kingston Inn. "The strangest thing happened the other day," Ivy had recently phoned to say. "There's a rosebush growing where that old gazebo used to be. Isn't that something !"

Whenever Angie thought of Julia, she wished her joy, just as she herself had found joy in her life with Gabriel. And whenever she remembered how he had come away from that adventure without a shred of scientific evidence to prove Julia's existence, she smiled.

She and Gabriel and Miles had gone through many adjustments in the past year: the move to Durham for Angie and Miles, the missing of family and friends, a new school for her son, and parenthood for Gabriel. But it had all worked out, thanks to time, love, and patience.

Angie and her son had made new friends, and they frequently visited their family and friends in Danville. Nila, Jake, and their little boy frequently came to spend long weekends in their home. Miles was flourishing socially and intellectually in the school for gifted children. And every day the bond between Miles and Gabriel grew stronger.

Angie lowered the book she had been reading and glanced over at her husband. He was slouched in the opposite corner of the new sofa she'd recently purchased for their home. He had not moved a muscle in at least twenty minutes.

He wore his "pondering" face, and as she watched him, a wave of desire rushed through her. She wanted to throw herself into his lap and kiss his sexy lower lip, which was characteristically poked out a bit.

Unbending one leg, she inched her foot toward him. "Gabe!" she shouted as she goosed his thigh with her toes.

"I can predict the ending of the book you're reading," he said, turning to smile at her.

"Oh?" She put down the romance novel and crawled over next to him. "How does it end?"

"They live happily ever after," he declared loftily. "Just like us."

His heart was in his smile. He raised his hands to cup her face and urged her closer.

"Happily ever after. Just like us," he whispered against her lips.

Angie smiled as she melted against him. In a moment or two, she'd share her wonderful news with him.

Gabriel opened his eyes wide as he continued to kiss his wife. *A baby!*

An image flashed through his mind. He saw an infant girl with his dark hair, her mother's dreamy blue eyes, and a smile as pure as Virginia sunshine.

THE EDITOR'S CORNER

Dear Readers,

If you loved our **BAD BOYS** last year, wait till you get a taste of our November LOVESWEPTs: **DANGEROUS MEN!** From a mysterious under-cover state trooper to a roguish football player and a wilder-than-wild oil field wildcatter, these men thrive on danger, live on the edge, and push passion right past the limit! Like our heroines, you'll find it impossible to resist the sheer thrill of a walk on the wild side with men who are definitely *not* what your mother had in mind! With bold seduction and promises of passion, November's six heroes will sweep our heroines—and you—off your feet and into the fantasy of being loved by a Dangerous Man. . . .

Leanne Banks has created our first Dangerous Man in the sultry tale she calls **DANCE WITH THE DEVIL**, LOVESWEPT #648. Garth Pendleton was a

ILLEGAL MOTION, LOVESWEPT #651, is as good as they come. Football star Nick Logan was desperate enough to try anything to clear his name, and he figured he could intimidate or charm the truth out of Willa Trask—until he was burned by the sparks that flared between him and the beautiful redhead! He'd hired her to rehabilitate his injured knee, vowing to discover if she'd helped frame him—but instead of an ice princess, he found in her a wanton witch who touched his soul. When you've read this winning story, I'm sure you'll become big fans of Donna Kauffman!

We turn from a rookie to an all-star pro for our next Dangerous Man. Let the heartbreaking emotion of Laura Taylor sweep you away with **WILDER'S WOMAN**, LOVESWEPT #652. Craig Wilder—uncivilized, untamed, he'd paid a high price for survival. He'd meant to teach Chelsea Lockridge a lesson, to punish his ex-wife for her betrayal, but he hadn't anticipated the erotic torment of molding his body to hers—nor imagined the tenderness still buried deep inside his battered heart! She'd braved the wilderness and a storm with evidence that could deliver the justice Craig had been denied, but Chelsea wanted to prove she'd never lost faith in him . . . or her reckless passion for the man who could make her purr with pleasure. Branded for all eternity by a lover whose scars ran deep, she vowed she could help Craig mourn the past and trust her again by fighting his demons with the sweet fury of her love. Laura's deeply moving tale will capture you, heart and soul.

If you like your men *truly* dangerous, Glenna McReynolds has the mystery man for you in **AVENGING ANGEL**, LOVESWEPT #653. Bruised and bloody, Dylan Jones has driven a thousand miles with her name on his lips, desperate to save Johanna Lane from being murdered! The secrets she knew made her bad boy who was definitely out of Erin Lindsey's league. Everything about him was a dare and Erin trembled at the danger of caring for a man whose darkest secret was tangled with her own shadowed past. Garth felt he'd waited for Erin forever and wanted to give her back her lost dreams, but if she knew the pain that haunted him, he feared the woman who'd slipped inside his lonely heart might slip away. This tempting tale is sure to please all of you who helped to make Leanne's January 1993 LOVESWEPT a #1 bestseller.

Doris Parmett's electrifying heroes and heroines have never been so highly-charged as they are in **BAD ATTITUDE**, LOVESWEPT #649. Reid Cameron was a heartbreaker cop who kissed like the hero of a hot romance. He'd invaded Polly Sweet's privacy—and her fantasies—when he'd commandeered her house to catch a jewel thief, but when he decided they'd play lovers and then tried to teach the feisty spitfire a lesson about feigning passion, both were shocked by the fireworks their lips set off! Doris is in top form with this sizzling story.

Longtime favorite author Patt Bucheister will tempt and tease you to distraction with her **TAME A WILDCAT**, LOVESWEPT #650. Ryder Knight had always thrived on the adventure of being a wildcatter, relished the pursuit of a new oil well, but he felt his restlessness vanish when Hannah Corbett told him he looked like trouble—and that he was no gentleman! But when his possessive embrace made her go up in flames, she feared losing control, trading her freedom for the joy only he could teach her. Patt will keep you on the edge of your seat for every page of this one!

We at LOVESWEPT are always pleased to welcome a talented new writer to our pages, and we're sure you'll agree that Donna Kauffman, author of a target, and he was her best chance of getting out alive—even if it meant abducting the lady and keeping her with him against her will. Frightened and furious, Johanna was stunned to realize she knew her captor . . . and once had even desired him! Dylan gambled his life to feel her heat and taste the forbidden fruit of her lips and Johanna longed to repay the debt. I can't think of a better way to end your month of **DANGEROUS MEN** than with Glenna's **AVENGING ANGEL**!

So hang on to your hearts—next month six **DANGEROUS MEN** are coming to steal them away!

Happy reading,

Nita Taublib

Nita Taublib

Associate Publisher

P.S. Don't miss the exciting women's fiction Bantam has coming in November—sensual seduction in Susan Johnson's **OUTLAW**; love and black magic over the centuries in **MOONLIGHT, MADNESS, AND MAGIC** by LOVESWEPT authors Suzanne Forster, Charlotte Hughes, and Olivia Rupprecht; and a classic Fayrene Preston romance, **SATIN AND STEELE**. We'll be giving you a sneak peek at these terrific books in next month's LOVESWEPTs. And immediately following this page, look for a preview of the spectacular women's fiction books from Bantam *available now!*

Don't miss these exciting books by your
favorite Bantam authors

On sale in September:
A WHISPER OF ROSES
by Teresa Medeiros

TENDER BETRAYAL
by Rosanne Bittner

THE PAINTED LADY
by Lucia Grahame

OREGON BROWN
by Sara Orwig

And in hardcover from Doubleday
SEIZED BY LOVE
by Susan Johnson

Teresa Medeiros

nationally bestselling author of
ONCE AN ANGEL
and HEATHER AND VELVET

presents

A WHISPER OF ROSES

"From humor to adventure, poignancy to passion, tenderness to sensuality, Teresa Medeiros writes rare love stories to cherish."—*Romantic Times*

Set in the wild Highlands of Scotland, this captivating historical romance is bursting with the breathtaking passion, sparkling humor, and enchanting atmosphere that have made Teresa Medeiros a bestselling author. It tells the heartbreaking tale of two lovers torn between their passion and the clan rivalry that divides their families.

The door behind him crashed open into the opposite wall, and Morgan swung around to find himself facing yet another exotic creature of myth.

A princess, her cloud of dark hair tumbled loose around her shoulders, the light behind her throwing every curve beneath her ivory nightdress into magnificent relief. Her delicate fingers were curled not around a scepter, but around the engraved hilt of a ceremonial claymore.

Silvery fingers of moonlight caressed the five feet of steel that lay between her hands and his heart.

"Hold your ground, rogue MacDonnell," she sweetly snarled. "One careless step and I'll be forced to take your head downstairs without the rest of you."

Morgan didn't even feel the pain as the crystal rose

snapped in his clumsy hands, embedding its stem deep in his palm.

"Why, you clumsy oaf! Look what you've gone and done now!"

Morgan's gaze automatically dropped to his hands. A jagged shard of glass protruded from his palm. Warm blood trickled down his wrist and forearm to puddle on one of Elizabeth Cameron's precious rugs. Before he could quench it, the old shame flared. Shame for being a MacDonnell. Shame for being such a crude ox. Just as quickly on its heels followed rage—the crushing rage that shielded his tattered pride from every blow. But before he could unleash it on the hapless girl, she dropped the sword and rushed over to him.

Tossing the splintered remains of the rose aside without a second glance, she cradled his hand in hers and dabbed at the wound with a wad of her nightdress. Her little hand was warm and soft and silky smooth beneath his own. "You really should take more care," she chided. "If you'd have struck your wrist, you might have bled to death."

Morgan was too dumbfounded by her concern to point out her illogic. If she'd have cut off his head, he might have bled to death even quicker. Still scowling over his hand, she dragged him toward the pale circle of light at the window.

"Be very still," she commanded. "I'm going to try to fish out this piece of glass. It's bound to be painful. You may scream if you like. I shan't think any less of you."

Since she'd never thought much of him to begin with, Morgan wasn't concerned. He didn't even flinch when she pressed his palm with her thumb and snagged the sliver of glass between the polished crescents of her fingernails.

Thoroughly bemused, Morgan studied her in the moonlight. The top of her head barely came to his chest. The spiral curls he used to yank with such relish tumbled down her back in inky waves. Her skin was fair except for the faintest hint of color, as if God had brushed rose petals across her cheeks and lips. A fringe of ebony silk shuttered her eyes. Her scent filled his nostrils, and he was shocked to feel his throat tighten with a primal hunger. She smelled like her mother, but fresher, sweeter. Some primitive male instinct warned him this was a bloom still on the vine, fragrant and tender and ripe. He frowned. She might be nectar to another man, but to him, Dougal Cameron's daughter would be as deadly as nightshade.

Her teeth cut into her lower lip as if to bite back a cry of her own as she drew forth the shard of glass and stanched the bleeding with yet another wad of her nightdress. Morgan feared he might soon have more of it twined around his arm than she had around her body. But an intriguing glimpse of a slender calf silenced his protest.

Grimacing, she lay the bloody splinter on the window-sill before glancing up at him.

At that moment, he cocked his head to the side, giving her an unobstructed view of his face. Moonlight melted over its harsh planes and angles, etching its alien virility in ruthless lines. He was a stranger, yet so hauntingly familiar she couldn't stop her hand from lifting, her fingertips from brushing the stubborn jut of his jaw. His eyes were guarded, like the forest at dusk.

"Hello, brat," he said.

Then she felt that old, familiar kick in the stomach and knew she was standing face to face in the moonlit tower with Morgan MacDonnell, his boyish promise of masculine beauty come to devastating fruition.

Mortified by her own boldness, she snatched her hand back, remembering another time she had touched him in tenderness and he had rubuked her in anger.

A wry grin touched his lips. "I suppose if you'd have known it was me, you'd have let me bleed to death."

Terrified she was going to revert to a stammering six-year-old, she snapped, "Of course not. You were dripping all over Mama's Flemish rug."

To hide her consternation, she lowered her gaze back to his hand. That was a mistake for she could not help staring, fascinated by the blunt size of his fingers, the warmth of his work-roughened skin, the rhythmic throb of his pulse beneath her thumb. She had the absurd thought that it must take a mighty heart indeed to fuel such a man.

"You've grown," she blurted out accusingly.

"So have you."

His low, amused tone warned her. She looked up to find his gaze taking a leisurely jaunt up her body, finally coming to rest with bold regard on her face. A splinter of anger twisted in her heart. For so long she had yearned for him to look at her with affection. But why now, when she sensed his admiration might be even more lethal to her than enmity?

Hardly aware of her actions, she tore a strip of priceless Chinese silk from her mother's drapes and wrapped it around his palm. "So what were you doing up here? Plotting a massacre? Trying to find a way to lower the harpsichord out the window? Searching for a mouse to put in my bed?"

Lucky mouse, Morgan thought, but he wisely refrained from saying so. "If you must know, lass, I was searchin' for a moment's peace."

"Ha!" She knotted the bandage with a crisp jerk that finally drew a flinch from him. "Peace and the MacDonnells hardly go hand in hand."

"Fine talk from a lass who just burst in here threatenin' to cut off my head."

Sabrina could hardly argue with the truth of that.

He jerked his head toward the door. "Why aren't you down there with the rest of your family, lordin' your noble gestures over the poor peasants?"

Morgan's size might have changed, but not the rest of him. Resenting his uncanny knack of making her feel ashamed of who she was, she gave a dainty snort. "Peasants, indeed. Barefoot savages, the lot of them. Mama would have been better off serving them at a trough instead of a table."

His voice was quiet, its very lack of emotion a rebuke of its own. "If their table manners aren't to your likin', it might be because most of them won't see that much food again in their lifetimes. And their feet are bare because they're savin' the rotted soles of their boots for the cold winter months. They don't lose as many toes that way."

Shame buffeted her. Sabrina dropped her gaze, then wished she hadn't as it fell on the stark lines of Morgan's bare legs and feet. Golden hair dusted his muscular calves. His soles must be as tough as leather to bear the stony soil of the mountainside without protection. Her own toes curled sheepishly into the plush cashmere of her stockings.

"I begged Mama to let me join the festivities," she confessed.

"Why didn't you appeal to your dotin' papa? As I recall,

he never could resist a flutter of those pretty little lashes of yours."

Sabrina's gaze shot to his face. Morgan had never given her any indication that he'd noticed her lashes before. "Even Papa was adamant this time." A soft chuckle escaped her. "It seems your reputations preceded you. He was terrified one of you might hit me over the head and drag me off by my hair."

Morgan was silent for so long that she feared she'd offended him again. Then he reached down and lifted a skein of her hair in his uninjured hand, rubbing it between thumb and forefinger. A dreamy languor stole across her features. The cadence of Sabrina's heartbeat shifted in warning.

He let the stolen tendril ripple through his fingers in a cascade of midnight silk before turning the dusky heat of his gaze on her. "I can't say I blame him, lass. If you were mine, I'd probably lock you away, too."

If you were mine . . .

The words hung suspended between them, far more awkward than their silence. In a breath of utter lunacy, Sabrina wondered how it would feel to belong to a man like him, dared to ponder what came after being dragged off by her hair.

Caught in the same spell of moonlight and solitude, Morgan's gaze dropped to her parted lips. His starving senses reeled, intoxicated by the scent of roses that flared his nostrils, the cling of her hair against his callused knuckles. He'd long ago resigned himself to the harsh life of a Highland warrior. But this girl's softness awakened old hungers and weakened his resolve. He hadn't touched a drop of wine, yet he felt drunk, reckless. What harm could one kiss do? Resisting the temptation to plunge his tongue between her unwitting lips, he leaned down and touched his mouth to hers.

At the press of Morgan's lips against her own, Sabrina's eyes fluttered shut. His kiss was brief, dry, almost tentative, yet a melting sweetness unfolded within her. She felt the leashed power in his touch. Such gentleness in a man his size wove a spell all its own. Only in the last brief second of contact did he allow himself the wicked luxury of dragging his lips across hers, molding her beneath him in perfect harmony.

TENDER BETRAYAL
by
ROSANNE BITTNER

Bestselling author of OUTLAW HEARTS
and THUNDER ON THE PLAINS

"Bittner's characters are so finely drawn, their lives so
richly detailed, one cannot help but to care deeply for
each of them." —*Affaire de Coeur*

*When Audra Brennan savored her first, forbidden taste of
desire in the arms of handsome lawyer Lee Jeffreys, his
caresses sparked a flame within that burned away the differences between rebel and Yankee.*

The shelling from the bigger guns seemed to have
stopped. She decided that at least until daylight she had no
choice but to stay here as Lee had directed. She went back
to the cot and lay down, breathing his scent on his pillow
and sheets. How odd that she felt so safe in this bed where
a Yankee soldier slept. She was in the center of the enemy
camp, yet she was not afraid.

She drifted off to sleep, losing all track of time. Finally
someone knocked gently on the rear door. "Audra? It's
me."

Audra rubbed at her eyes, holding the shirt around
herself as she found her way to the door. It was still dark.
"Lee?"

"Let me in. The worst is over."

Audra obeyed, and Lee turned and latched the door
again. Audra looked up at him, seeing blood on his right
arm. "You're hurt!"

"Nothing drastic. I told my commander I'd tend to it

myself. He doesn't know you're in here, and I don't want him to know just yet." He threw a bundle of clothes on the small table on which the lamp was sitting. "I looted those out of a clothing store like a common thief. I don't know your size. I just took a guess. You've got to have something to wear when you leave here."

Lee removed his jacket and boots, then began unbuttoning his shirt. "It's a madhouse out there. Most of the men have chased the rebels back into the countryside, and they're looting through town like crazy men. It's practically impossible to keep any of these men in line. They aren't regular army, just civilian volunteers, for the most part, come here to teach the rebels a lesson. They don't know a damn thing about real military conduct or how to obey orders." He glanced at her. "I still intend to have the bastards who attacked you whipped. How do you feel?"

She sat down on the cot, suddenly self-conscious now that she was more rested. She had removed her shoes and stockings and wore only his shirt and her bloomers. "Just terribly tired and . . . I don't know . . . numb, I guess. It's all so ugly and unreal."

"That's war, Audra, ugly and unreal. You asked me once what it's like. Now you know." He peeled off his bloodstained shirt, and Audra found herself studying his muscular arms and the familiar broad chest, the dark hair that lightly dusted that chest and led downward in a V shape past the belt of his pants. He walked to the stand that still held a bowl of water and he poured some fresh water into it, then wet a rag and held it to the cut on his arm, which was already scabbing over. "Some rebel tried to stab me with his bayonet. Missed what he was aiming for by a long shot, but he didn't miss me all together, obviously."

"Let me help you."

"Don't worry about it. It isn't bleeding anymore." He washed his face and neck, then dried off and picked up a flask of whiskey. He opened it and poured some over the cut, grimacing at the sting of it. Then he swallowed some of the whiskey straight from the flask. "They say whiskey is supposed to help ease pain," he said then. "It does, but only physical pain. It doesn't do a thing for the pain in a man's heart."

She looked away. "Lee, don't—"

"Why not? In a couple of days you'll go back to Brennan Manor, and I'll go on with what I have to do, because I'm bound to do it and it isn't in me to be a deserter, no matter the reason. You have to stay near home because it's the only way you're going to know what happened to Joey, and you'll want to be there when he comes home, God willing. Who knows what will happen when all this is over? In the meantime I've found you again, and I need to tell you I love you, Audra. I never stopped loving you and I probably never will."

Audra held back tears. Why was he saying this now, when it was impossible for them to be together? Everything had changed. They were not the same people as they'd been that summer at Maple Shadows, and besides that, it was wrong to be sitting here half-undressed in front of the man she'd slept with while married to someone else, wasn't it? It was wrong to care this much about a Yankee. *All* of this was wrong, but then, what was right anymore?

He set the flask down on the table. "This might really be it, Audra; the end for you and me. But we have tonight."

"Why is it always that way for us? It was like that at Maple Shadows, and that one night you came to visit. All we ever have is one night, Lee, never knowing what will come tomorrow. I can't do that again. It hurts too much, and it's wrong."

Audra looked away as Lee began to undress. "Please take me somewhere, Lee, anywhere away from here."

He came over to kneel in front of her, grasping her wrists. "There *is* no place to take you, not tonight. And it's *not* wrong, Audra. It was *never* wrong, and you know it. And this time it isn't just tonight. When this is over, I'm coming back, and we're going to be together, do you hear me? I'm not going to live like this the rest of my life. I want you, Audra, and dammit, you want *me*! We've both known it since that first day you came here to see me, widow or not! Maybe this *is* the last chance we'll have to be together, but as God is my witness, if I don't get killed or so badly wounded that I can't come to you, I'll be back to find you, and we're going to put this war behind us!"

She looked at him pleadingly. "That's impossible now," she said in a near whisper.

"That isn't true. You just don't want to *believe* that it's possible, because it makes you feel like a traitor." He leaned closer. "Well, then, *I'm* a traitor, too! Because while my men are out there chasing and killing rebels, I'll be in here making *love* to one!"

Why couldn't she object, argue, remember why she should say no? Why was she never able to resist this man she should have hated?

"I never said anything about making love," she whispered.

He searched her green eyes, eyes that had told him all along how much she wanted him again. "You didn't have to," he answered.

THE PAINTED LADY

by

LUCIA GRAHAME

This is a stunningly sensual first novel about sexual awakening set in nineteenth-century France and England. Romantic Times *called it "a unique and rare reading experience."*

This wonderfully entertaining novel showcases the superb writing talents of Lucia Grahame. With lyric simplicity and beauty THE PAINTED LADY *will entrance you from first page to last. Read on to discover an exquisite story about a proud, dark-haired woman and her hidden desire that is finally freed.*

"If I stay longer with you tonight," Anthony said, his words seeming to reach me through a thick mist, "it will be on one condition. You will not balk at *anything* I ask of you. I leave it to you. I will go now and count tonight to your account, since, although you were occasionally dilatory, you acquitted yourself well enough, for the most part. Or I will stay, on *my* conditions—but at *your* wish. It rests with you. Do I stay or go?"

"Stay," I whispered.

I swayed and jingled as he led me back to the hearthside and laid me down upon the pillows.

"Undress me," he commanded when we were stretched out before the fire. "Slowly. As slowly as you can."

I moved closer to him and began to unfasten the buttons of his waistcoat.

He sighed.

"Don't rush," he whispered. "I can feel how eager you are, but try to control yourself. Take your time."

It was maddening to force myself to that unhurried

pace, but in the end it only sharpened my hunger. As I contemplated the climactic pleasures in store—who could have said how long it would take to achieve them?—I could not help savoring the small but no less sweet ones immediately at hand. The slight drag against my skin of the fine wool that clothed him, more teasing even than I had imagined it; the almost imperceptible fragrance of lavender that wafted from his shirt, the hands which lay so lightly upon my waist as I absorbed the knowledge that the task he had set for me was not an obstacle to fulfillment but a means of enhancing it.

Yet I had unbuttoned only his waistcoat and his shirt when he told me to stop. He drew back from me a little. The very aura of controlled desire he radiated made me long to submerge myself in the impersonal heat and forgetfulness that his still presence next to me both promised and withheld.

I moved perhaps a centimeter closer to him.

"No," he said.

He began, in his calm, unhasty way, to remove his remaining clothing himself. I steadied my breath a little and watched the firelight move like a sculptor's fingers over his cool, hard body.

At last he leaned over me, but without touching me.

"You're so compliant tonight," he said almost tenderly. "You must be very hungry for your freedom, *mon fleur du miel*."

I felt a twist of sadness. For an instant, I thought he had used Frederick's nickname for me. But he had called me something quite different—a flower, not of evil, but of sweetness . . . honey.

He brought his hand to my cheek and stroked it softly. I closed my eyes. Only the sudden sharp intake of my breath could have told him of the effect of that light touch.

He bent his head. I caught the scents of mint and smoke and my own secrets as his mouth moved close to mine.

I tipped my head back and opened my lips.

How long I had resisted those kisses! Now I craved his mouth, wanting to savor and prolong every sensation that could melt away my frozen, imprisoning armor of misery and isolation.

He barely grazed my lips with his.

Then he pulled himself to his knees and gently coaxed me into the same position, facing him.

Keeping his lips lightly on mine, he reached out and took my shoulders gently to bring me closer. My breasts brushed his chest with every long, shivering breath I took.

"You are free now," whispered my husband at last, releasing me, "to do as you like. . . . How will you use your liberty?"

For an answer, I put my arms around his neck, sank back upon the pillows, pulling him down to me, and brought my wild mouth to his. . . .

OREGON BROWN
by
SARA ORWIG

Bestselling author of TIDES OF PASSION
and NEW ORLEANS

"The multi-faceted talent of Sara Orwig gleams as
bright as gold." —*Rave Reviews*

*With more than five million copies of her books in print,
Sara Orwig is without a doubt one of romance's top authors.
Her previous novels have been showered with praise and
awards, including five* Romantic Times *awards and nu-
merous* Affaire de Coeur *awards.*

*Now Bantam Books is proud to present a new edition of one
of her most passionate novels—the story of a woman forced to
choose between fantasy and reality. . . .*

Charity Webster left the city for small-town Oklahoma
to assume the reins of the family company she had
inherited. With nothing behind her but a failed business and a shattered romance, and no one in her new
life except an aging aunt, Charity gives her nights to a
velvet-voiced late-night deejay . . . and to a fantasy
about the man behind the sexy, sultry voice.

But daylight brings her into head-on conflict with
another man, the wealthy O. O. Brown, who is maneu-
vering to acquire the family firm. Arrogant and all too
aware of his own charm, he still touches off a sensuous
spark in Charity that she can't deny . . . and she finds
herself torn between two men—one a mystery, the
other the keeper of her deepest secrets.

OFFICIAL RULES

To enter the sweepstakes below carefully follow all instructions found elsewhere in this offer.

The **Winners Classic** will award prizes with the following approximate maximum values: 1 Grand Prize: $26,500 (or $25,000 cash alternate); 1 First Prize: $3,000; 5 Second Prizes: $400 each; 35 Third Prizes: $100 each; 1,000 Fourth Prizes: $7.50 each. Total maximum retail value of Winners Classic Sweepstakes is $42,500. Some presentations of this sweepstakes may contain individual entry numbers corresponding to one or more of the aforementioned prize levels. To determine the Winners, individual entry numbers will first be compared with the winning numbers preselected by computer. For winning numbers not returned, prizes will be awarded in random drawings from among all eligible entries received. Prize choices may be offered at various levels. If a winner chooses an automobile prize, all license and registration fees, taxes, destination charges and, other expenses not offered herein are the responsibility of the winner. If a winner chooses a trip, travel must be complete within one year from the time the prize is awarded. Minors must be accompanied by an adult. Travel companion(s) must also sign release of liability. Trips are subject to space and departure availability. Certain black-out dates may apply.

The following applies to the sweepstakes named above:

No purchase necessary. You can also enter the sweepstakes by sending your name and address to: P.O. Box 508, Gibbstown, N.J. 08027. Mail each entry separately. Sweepstakes begins 6/1/93. Entries must be received by 12/30/94. Not responsible for lost, late, damaged, misdirected, illegible or postage due mail. Mechanically reproduced entries are not eligible. All entries become property of the sponsor and will not be returned.

Prize Selection/Validations: Selection of winners will be conducted no later than 5:00 PM on January 28, 1995, by an independent judging organization whose decisions are final. Random drawings will be held at 1211 Avenue of the Americas, New York, N.Y. 10036. Entrants need not be present to win. Odds of winning are determined by total number of entries received. Circulation of this sweepstakes is estimated not to exceed 200 million. All prizes are guaranteed to be awarded and delivered to winners. Winners will be notified by mail and may be required to complete an affidavit of eligibility and release of liability which must be returned within 14 days of date on notification or alternate winners will be selected in a random drawing. Any prize notification letter or any prize returned to a participating sponsor, Bantam Doubleday Dell Publishing Group, Inc., its participating divisions or subsidiaries, or the independent judging organization as undeliverable will be awarded to an alternate winner. Prizes are not transferable. No substitution for prizes except as offered or as may be necessary due to unavailability, in which case a prize of equal or greater value will be awarded. Prizes will be awarded approximately 90 days after the drawing. All taxes are the sole responsibility of the winners. Entry constitutes permission (except where prohibited by law) to use winners' names, hometowns, and likenesses for publicity purposes without further or other compensation. Prizes won by minors will be awarded in the name of parent or legal guardian.

Participation: Sweepstakes open to residents of the United States and Canada, except for the province of Quebec. Sweepstakes sponsored by Bantam Doubleday Dell Publishing Group, Inc., (BDD), 1540 Broadway, New York, NY 10036. Versions of this sweepstakes with different graphics and prize choices will be offered in conjunction with various solicitations or promotions by different subsidiaries and divisions of BDD. Where applicable, winners will have their choice of any prize offered at level won. Employees of BDD, its divisions, subsidiaries, advertising agencies, independent judging organization, and their immediate family members are not eligible.

Canadian residents, in order to win, must first correctly answer a time limited arithmetical skill testing question. Void in Puerto Rico, Quebec and wherever prohibited or restricted by law. Subject to all federal, state, local and provincial laws and regulations. For a list of major prize winners (available after 1/29/95): send a self-addressed, stamped envelope entirely separate from your entry to: Sweepstakes Winners, P.O. Box 517, Gibbstown, NJ 08027. Requests must be received by 12/30/94. DO NOT SEND ANY OTHER CORRESPONDENCE TO THIS P.O. BOX.

SWP 7/93

Don't miss these fabulous Bantam women's fiction titles Now on sale

• A WHISPER OF ROSES

by **Teresa Medeiros,** author of HEATHER AND VELVET
A tantalizing romance of love and treachery that sweeps from a medieval castle steeped in splendor to a crumbling Scottish fortress poised high above the sea. ___29408-3 $5.50/6.50 in Canada

• TENDER BETRAYAL

by **Rosanne Bittner,** author of OUTLAW HEARTS
The powerful tale of a Northern lawyer who falls in love with a beautiful plantation owner's daughter, yet willingly becomes the instrument of her family's destruction when war comes to the South. ___29808-9 $5.99/6.99 in Canada

• THE PAINTED LADY

by **Lucia Grahame**
"A unique and rare reading experience." —Romantic Times
In the bestselling tradition of Susan Johnson comes a stunningly sensual novel about sexual awakening set in 19th-century France and England. ___29864-X $4.99/5.99 in Canada

• OREGON BROWN

by **Sara Orwig,** author of NEW ORLEANS
A classic passionate romance about a woman forced to choose between fantasy and reality. ___56088-3 $4.50/5.50 in Canada

Ask for these books at your local bookstore or use this page to order.

❑ Please send me the books I have checked above. I am enclosing $ _____ (add $2.50 to cover postage and handling). Send check or money order, no cash or C. O. D.'s please.

Name _____

Address _____

City/ State/ Zip _____

Send order to: Bantam Books, Dept. FN117, 2451 S. Wolf Rd., Des Plaines, IL 60018
Allow four to six weeks for delivery.
Prices and availability subject to change without notice.

FN117 10/93